The Sweet Spot

Arlington Aces 2

Elley Arden

Adams Media

New York   London   Toronto   Sydney   New Delhi

CRIMSON

Crimson Romance
An Imprint of Simon & Schuster, Inc.
1230 Avenue of the Americas
New York, NY 10020

ISBN 978-1-4405-9153-2
ISBN 978-1-4405-9154-9 (ebook)

*To all the baseball couples whose love has survived
despite the stress and distance.*

Chapter One

Giovanni Caceres had seen a lot of crazy shit go down in locker rooms, but this was the first time he'd been greeted by a blow-up doll wearing his jersey.

He turned his back on the buxom plastic lady with the oversized mouth and scanned the room's guilty occupants. They were fresh from morning practice. When did they have time to pull this off?

A few guys snickered but didn't make eye contact.

"Okay. Which one of you assholes misplaced your date?" he asked. "Pratt? This has your name written all over it."

"No way, man. She's got *your name* on her jersey. She must've heard you've been having trouble scoring." Catcher Ian Pratt stuffed his head into his locker, where his laughter echoed.

Giovanni stopped playing hard ass and laughed, too. He never had trouble scoring on field or off. He dropped his duffle bag and grabbed the doll, pulling her into a dramatic embrace. "*¿Cómo te llamas?*" he cooed as he rubbed her cold, latex bottom. His teammates egged him on with whistles and catcalls.

He raised a hand to her breast and gave it a squeeze as he leaned in and pretended to be listening to her. "What's that?" After a beat filled with more harassment from his teammates, he gasped like she'd said something scandalous. "Pratt, I didn't know you had a sister."

The clubhouse rattled with raucous laughter, but the revelry quieted almost immediately, leaving behind an eerie silence.

Slowly, he lowered the doll and looked to the door, chagrined and expecting to see Pauly Byrne standing there. Coach's calls for a "more sensitive locker-room environment" on behalf of their star pitcher, the Independence League's first female player, hadn't exactly fallen on deaf ears but ... well, they were still in the adjustment stage. It wasn't Pauly at the door, though.

No, it was Rachel Reed.

The team's owner drilled her stone-cold eyes straight at him. "Come with me, Mr. Caceres." Then she glanced at the doll. "And leave your friend behind."

Shit. Giovanni propped the doll against his locker and left the room amid quiet jeers. Pissing off Reed wasn't on his list of goals for his third season with the Aces.

"Sorry about that," he said, sheepishly.

Rachel waited until the locker-room door closed behind him, and then she turned on him in the empty hall. "I'm glad you're sorry, because that will make this a whole lot easier." She flashed a satisfied grin. "Sam has been called away on a family emergency, and that's unfortunate because he was supposed to be giving a batting lesson in the cages in five minutes. Since it's too late to cancel, you're going to fill in for him."

"Batting lessons? Like, to a kid?" Not that Giovanni didn't like kids, but coaching Little Leaguers wasn't on his list of goals either.

"To my *niece*." She stressed that last word. "So don't screw up. Watch your mouth. Keep it clean. And take it seriously."

"I thought she played softball." He'd seen the kid hanging around a few times over the last two years, and had a vague memory of the girl's eyeball-searing lime green Arlington Softball Association T-shirt.

"Not anymore. She wants to be the next Pauly Byrne." She caught his reflexive eye roll and her own pupils narrowed. "Do you have a problem with that?"

"No, sir. Uh, ma'am!" he gulped. "No, ma'am."

"Good."

"But, uh, why not get Pauly ... ma'am, uh, boss," he added quickly. "I mean, I don't have any experience with kids, and with all respect, I really gotta be concentrating on my own game right now. I mean, I got big plans. I figure if I want to make it out of indie ball—"

Rachel's long, lean body stiffened, and her eyes narrowed to slits. "Pauly is busy at the moment. You, on the other hand, seem to have plenty of time to … practice your pick-up skills, so I'm sure you would be just thrilled to donate some of that abundant free time to help inspire and motivate one of this community's young athletes, wouldn't you?"

"Well, actually, I was just—"

Rachel leaned closer, her glare going even steelier.

"Let me also remind you that your *big plans* require my participation, if not my approval. Isn't that correct?"

Unfortunately. He was under contract, which meant the Aces owned him. Rachel owned him. If a minor league team came sniffing around, she would have the final word. "Correct," he said, defeated.

"Then you'll do this, and you'll do it well—until I say you're done doing it. Am I clear?"

He clenched his jaw. Why did that sound like he was signing on for more than one lesson? "Crystal."

"Good. I'm glad we're on the same page." Her posture relaxed, but her eyes stayed sharp. "I'd say I want a full report after the lesson, but I'm sure Macy will give me the rundown—and she doesn't leave out details."

"Great," he said with only a hint of sarcasm.

She pivoted, stalking off, and Gio waited, only letting out a frustrated sigh once he could no longer hear her heels clicking on the concrete floors. He rubbed a hand over his face. This entire day felt like some sort of setup. He was almost afraid to head to the cages to see what was waiting for him next.

He shook his head, feeling stupid. Was he really afraid of a preteen? Besides, what was a few hours hitting balls to the boss lady's niece? Maybe it would get him on her good side if the kid gave him a thumbs-up.

His dark mood lifted. A little charity work might earn him his ticket back to the big leagues.

For good, this time.

• • •

"Right there," Macy said. "That's him."

Helen Anne Reed swung her freshly washed and waxed Range Rover into a parking spot at Federal Field and eyed up the man candy hauling a bucket of balls toward the batting cages her daughter was pointing out.

From this distance and behind the darkened lenses of her Ray-Bans, Helen Anne couldn't make out his finer details—just the big picture. The sculpted muscles in his arms and legs. The power in his stride. The healthy head of dark hair glistening in the sun as it ruffled in the early-spring breeze.

"Mom?"

She blinked at the sound of her twelve-year-old's impatient voice. "Yes?"

"Why is your mouth open? Are you looking at him funny?" Macy asked.

Helen Anne pressed her lips together and closed her eyes behind the shield of her sunglasses and said, "I wasn't looking at him funny. I was just trying to figure out if that was actually him."

"Mom," Macy said with a middle school sized proportion of exasperation. "He's been on the Aces for two seasons already! You know what he looks like."

Oh, she did. But she was used to seeing him way out in center field, covered from head to toe in baseball gear. Not in an Aces' T-shirt with cut off sleeves that dipped low enough to show off a shadow of pec.

Sun's out guns out, she thought, borrowing a frat boy phrase from a young adult novel she'd recently read, and then she promptly made a face, because, at thirty-six years old, she had no business thinking such things. What had gotten into her today?

"Mom, are you okay?" Macy asked.

"I'm fine. Absolutely fine. I'm just thinking … about the bookstore … and grandpa … and PTA. I have a lot on my mind."

Like the fact that her sister thought Giovanni Caceres was the answer to Helen Anne's latest dilemma. *Dear God!* If she couldn't manage to ogle the man gracefully from a distance, how was she going to approach him and ask him to be her partner for Macy's middle school fundraiser?

As PTA president-elect and co-chair of Dancing with the Arlington Middle School Stars, Helen Anne couldn't exactly decline to participate in the dance contest, even though she wanted to more than anything. Her idea of excitement was a *Downton Abbey* marathon and a bottle of Chardonnay, not dressing up in a poodle skirt to jitterbug with a baseball hotshot who had once been dubbed "God's gift to ballroom," according to her sister.

"Can I go?" Macy's eyes shined as she lifted the baseball bat from between her thighs. The skinny end of the bat was threaded through a gap at the wrist end of the glove Rachel and Sam had given her as a birthday present a few months ago when she'd announced she was giving up softball. Helen Anne still wasn't thrilled with the idea. Baseball seemed like an uphill battle for a girl, one that would be filled with ridicule and unwanted attention. But Macy didn't want to hear about that.

"It's not too late to change your mind," Helen Anne said, ever hopeful.

"How many times do I have to tell you? I don't want to change my mind." Macy's voice went shrill. "I want to be like Pauly. Why can't you just be okay with that?"

Maybe because those words—*I want to be like Pauly*—sounded an awful lot like *I don't want to be anything like you.*

Helen Anne sighed. "Go ahead. Please be respectful and pay attention. If you need me, I'll be right here with my book." She held up a weathered copy of *The Age of Innocence*. Trying to work up enough courage to approach the man after the lesson was over.

Macy shot out of the car without hesitation and jogged across the recently lined asphalt toward the batting cages. She didn't offer a backward glance.

Helen Anne's gaze slid to Giovanni. He bent over a bucket of balls outside the cage, and the silky fabric of his court shorts pulled across his taut ass. She repositioned the air-conditioning vents to feel the full force on her face. Maybe she shouldn't have let Rachel talk her into this. Maybe it wasn't too late to stick with her original plan and ask Lester Birdwell to be her partner. Lester wouldn't help her make any post-divorce social statements, but he would donate ice cream for the refreshment table. Birdwell Creamery did have the best maple walnut in town.

The message indicator on Helen Anne's phone chimed, and she looked down at a text notification from Stacy Deacon, her friend and co-chair.

She propped her phone on the steering wheel and opened the text:

Lester Birdwell is dancing with Ariel, and he's donating three flavors of ice cream WITH sprinkles!!!! How cool is that?!?!

It wasn't cool at all. Now Helen Anne's back was against the proverbial wall. How would it look if the PTA president-elect couldn't find a dance partner?

With a grunt, she pushed that depressing thought out of her head and typed the word "Awesome," making sure to add a smiley face.

She needed to suck it up and ask Giovanni.

As if Rachel could sense Helen Anne's struggle, the phone vibrated again, and a picture of Rachel cheek-to-cheek with Macy popped up on the screen of Helen Anne's phone.

She pressed the hands-free calling button on her steering wheel and said, "Are you checking up on me?"

"Yes. Did you ask him?"

"Not yet. I haven't been out of the car. I'll do it after the lesson is over."

"You're stalling."

"Probably. But at this point, I'm not going to interrupt the lesson. Macy'll kill me." She blew out a deep breath. "How's Sam's dad?" Rachel's boyfriend's father had been rushed to the emergency room early that morning.

"The chest pains have subsided, but they're running tests and keeping him overnight. I'll let you know the results as soon as I get an update." Her sister's no-nonsense voice took on a petulant tone. "Wouldn't it suck if it was a heart attack? I mean, Paul has the biggest heart of anyone I know. He doesn't deserve that."

Helen Anne bristled. "People don't always get what they deserve, Rach. It's not like Dad deserved to get Alzheimer's."

But, secretly, in her more cynical moments, Helen Anne *had* thought it grimly ironic that a man who'd spent most of his life away from his family in pursuit of wealth and professional success would end up eventually forgetting he'd had any family at all.

"True."

"And it's not like I deserved to be thirty-six and divorced." She tried to keep a note of defensiveness out of her voice, but she didn't quite succeed.

"Well, that depends on how you look at it. The way I see it, you deserved to get divorced because you deserve someone way better than Jeremy Gardner."

"I don't want to talk about Jeremy," she said, churlish now.

"Then let's talk about Giovanni and how you can get your ass out of that car and claim the only dance partner in Arlington who's going to help you make a damn statement to this town." Helen rolled her eyes, but a grin was starting to tug at her lips. "Helen Anne Reed is no failure. She's more than Jeremy Gardner's ex-wife. And she's tired of all the damn pity. Can I get a hell yeah?"

Helen Anne chuckled. "Hell yeah." The irony of her high-powered workaholic sister giving her a pep talk on getting more out of life was sort of rich. Rachel had definitely changed since she'd reluctantly come back to Arlington to help Dad with the team, and Helen Anne was forever grateful they'd gotten the chance to mend fences, but it was still hard to believe.

"Atta girl. You want more out of life right?"

"Absolutely."

"Then get out of the car and ask that man to dance. Trust me. He won't say no. I have him by the balls."

Crunch!

There was an airy pop. The sound of something expanding. A loud, crackling noise that snapped Helen Anne's head up and widened her eyes.

In the middle of her windshield sat a crater of displaced glass, and in the middle of that, as if it belonged there, sat a baseball.

"What was that?" Rachel asked.

"Fate," Helen Anne said, making sure she got out of the car. And if that weren't enough, it seemed she had Giovanni by the balls now, too.

• • •

Giovanni glanced at the child by his side. Her wide eyes and O-shaped mouth said he was in big trouble.

"That's my mom's car," she said.

Great. Rachel was going to love this. How had he managed to find the needle in the haystack of a mostly empty parking lot?

"You should've been in the batting cage," Macy said.

"I know that now." He also knew he wasn't as good at demonstrating the direction of the ball off the bat as he assumed himself to be.

"Here she comes!" Macy covered her mouth with her mitt.

Face the music, his father would say. But it wouldn't be easy, considering Giovanni and Reece had just paid rent, and he was now sitting on $78.32 in his checking account back in San Diego. How much did it cost to fix a windshield? No idea. He didn't even own a car.

Giovanni walked toward the woman with Macy by his side and called out an apology. "I was … "

"Trying to teach me to get under the ball." The kid ran ahead and wrapped her arms around her mother's waist. "I'm so sorry, Mom. I didn't mean to hit it so hard."

The woman lifted the little girl's ball cap and after some hushed words spoken with a stern face, kissed the child on the forehead.

He was confused. Flushed with a guilty man's heartbeat. Very aware that the woman in front of him was Rachel's sister, and one way or another, word would get back to her. Talk about screwing up.

"Is the damage bad?" he asked.

Helen Anne looked up, made eye contact, and something gripped him by the throat. No words. Only the thought that, up close, she wasn't what he'd expected. This woman wasn't much taller than her daughter, with long, brown curls framing a beautifully rounded face that matched the lush curves of her body. She looked soft and sexy in some ruffled, flowery thing that clung to her in all the right places.

"It'll need to be replaced," she said coolly with her arms still wrapped around her daughter's shoulders.

"I'm so sorry," the little girl said again, tugging on her mother's arms.

"I'm the one who's sorry." But before he got any further, Helen Anne shifted her attention to the phone in her hand.

"Excuse me for a minute, please. I have to take this." And then to her daughter she said, "It's Grandma."

Now Giovanni had time to stew about screwing up when Rachel had told him specifically not to. The blow-up doll had been good, not-so-clean fun. But the windshield? That had been carelessness. Bad decision-making. And he needed to watch it, moving forward. Any more and people might start thinking he was up to his old tricks. He'd spent the last two years making serious strides.

He nudged the child beside him. "Why did you tell your mom you did it?"

"Because I don't like when people fight." The corners of her blue eyes dipped, and he got the distinct impression she was speaking from considerable experience.

That didn't sit right with him.

He glanced at the pretty, put-together woman, who was still on the phone, and wondered if "pretty" and "put-together" weren't synonymous with "uptight" and "control freak." Still, she didn't look like the kind of woman who went around shredding people.

"I'm not going to fight with your mom." That would be crazy-ass stupid.

Macy studied him from beneath the brim of her Arlington Aces baseball cap. Suspicion twisted her lips.

Man, somebody had done a number on this kid.

He traced an "x" over his heart and said, "I promise. I don't like when people fight either." Not anymore at least. Not in the last two years for sure. "It's cool you want to take the rap for me, but I can't let you do it."

"Yeah, you can."

He smiled. Were all kids her age this feisty?

"If you fight about the windshield, she's just going to force me to go back to softball."

He didn't exactly follow that reasoning. "What's wrong with softball?" he asked. After all, if the kid went back to softball, he would be off the coaching hook.

She rolled her eyes in a way that said, *Not you too*. "I like baseball more. It's faster, and I wanna prove I'm good enough to play with the guys, and maybe then ... " Her face puckered like she'd chewed and swallowed a mouthful of sour candies. She looked away. "Never mind. I just like it more."

Okay, but she still looked bothered. In fact, her eyes glistened with unshed tears. He didn't need the kid crying on top of everything else. "Too late," he said. "You started talking. Now you gotta finish. You said, 'And maybe then ... ' what?" He tapped the bat to the tip of her sneaker to encourage her.

"Maybe then they won't be so mean." She looked away again. "Maybe they'll like me and we can be friends."

The memories stirred a dormant anger in his belly. Giovanni planted the bat between his feet and crouched so he and Macy were eye to watery eye. "When I was your age, people made fun of me, too," he said. "I tried to handle it alone, but it led me into some pretty dark places. You need to talk to an adult about this. Adults can help."

"Not my mom. She'll just make me quit baseball." She gave him a hard look. "Why did people make fun of you?"

He glanced at the woman, who was still pacing the parking lot with her phone to her ear, and wished she would hurry up. Things were getting a little too personal here, and he was wasting time that could be spent working on his own baseball skills. But then he glanced back at the little girl, who was waiting patiently, and he figured after shattering her mother's windshield, the least he could do was help her avoid his fate.

"People made fun of me because I used to be a dancer," he said.

Her right eyebrow crooked in disbelief. "Really?"

"Yep. When I was your age, my family travelled all over the world, performing for lots of different people."

"What kind of dance?"

"All kinds. But my favorite was salsa," he said, unleashing his Spanish accent and making her giggle. "I liked to rumba, too." And that had gotten his ass kicked more times than he could count—until he'd learned to fight back.

"So like *Dancing with the Stars* stuff?"

"Exactly."

"Cool." She quieted for a minute and stared off in the direction of her mother, then she looked at him with a mischievous smile that showed off a missing upper tooth. "Did you wear those sparkly, low-cut shirts?" She wrinkled her nose and giggled again.

"Would you make fun of me if I did?" Because a lot of guys had, and it still left a bad taste in his mouth.

Her expression turned serious. "No. I don't make fun of anyone."

"Good." He bounced on his knees a couple times and then stood. "And those boys shouldn't be making fun of anyone either, so talk to somebody."

Out of the corner of his eye, he saw her mother walking towards them. Her hips were swinging, and her long locks fluttered in the warm breeze. She looked deep in thought but not angry, and an inexplicable awareness shot through him again.

"I'm going to tell her the truth." Before Macy could complain, he added, "I got this. Don't worry."

The woman stopped short of where he stood on the curb and tilted her head to one side. "Sorry about that." The sun blasted her face, forcing her to shield her eyes.

He squared his shoulders and accepted his fate. "I broke your windshield."

She narrowed her gaze and straightened her head. Then she dropped the hand that was doubling as a visor and looked at her daughter. "You said you did it."

Macy looked at Giovanni with a whole lot of doubt wrinkling her face.

"She was covering for me, but I can't let her take the blame," he said, forcing a smile, hoping to use the good looks God had given him to gain an edge. "It was me, and I'll pay for the damage."

"That won't be necessary." The woman's beautiful but blank face and even tone made her thoughts unreadable.

"I insist."

"My sister owns this team," she said, a glint of pity in her eyes. "I know you guys don't make a lot of money."

Ouch. A man didn't like to be reminded of his shortcomings, and Giovanni's bank account was definitely short these days. His ego was still trying to recover when she added, "But maybe you could work it off."

He straightened with interest, even puffed out his chest. If this had been a few years ago and she had been anybody other than the team owner's snobby sister, he could've been easily persuaded to work it off any way she could imagine. But this woman couldn't possibly be thinking the same thing. Her skirt fell below her knees, and her shirt was buttoned to her throat. She was too straitlaced conservative to risk him wrinkling her 3000-thread-count sheets.

"What did you have in mind?" he asked.

"Dance with me." Her cheeks pinked and her eyes widened like she was asking for something scandalous.

Then she flicked a glance at Macy, who hissed at his side, "Yes!" With a fist pump. "That would be so cool."

Helen Anne's smile wobbled. "It's for her school's fundraiser."

Giovanni felt the rest of his free time, which was supposed to be devoted to polishing his baseball skills, slipping away. He didn't have time to coach this little girl *and* teach her mother to dance.

"My sister said you can dance, and it's always advantageous for the team to be represented in community events, so ... "

Giovanni smelled a rat. But when the rat owned your baseball team and held your future in her hands, what choice did you have?

Chapter Two

Two days later, Helen Anne was back at Federal Field, where the sun blazed through the glass rotunda like it had through her brand-new windshield.

"Where are you taking me?" her father asked, and he hesitated as the elevator doors slid open.

These three-times-a-week trips to the stadium gave her mother a much-needed break from taking care of a man with progressing Alzheimer's, and her father a chance to look and feel like his old self again.

He was dressed in an Aces' polo shirt and tan slacks. His salt-and-pepper hair was neatly combed, and his aged-but-handsome face was shaved. He fussed with his prized Rolex, which sat snug on his left wrist.

"We're at the baseball field, Daddy. You're going to help Rachel get ready for the new season." And Helen Anne was going to meet Giovanni for her first dance lesson.

The blueberry muffin she'd eaten for breakfast churned in her stomach.

She couldn't believe she was making time for something this crazy in her already crowded schedule. The white board calendar in her office at the bookstore and the duplicate in the pantry at home couldn't keep track of any more. The hours she would be at the store. The hours she would be at the school. The hours she would be at the house sitting with her father or attending doctor's appointments. And now, the hours Macy would be at baseball practices and games, and the hours Helen Anne would be at dance practice—of all the ridiculous things. Just thinking about those overwritten squares made her palms clammy. Or maybe that was the idea of dancing with Giovanni.

Danny stepped into the elevator, and more lines wrinkled his face. "I own a baseball team," he said.

Whether it had been in an effort to inform her or remind himself, she agreed. Technically, Rachel owned the team, but Dr. Rictor had told the family early on that it was best to let Danny believe whatever he wanted to believe rather than agitate him.

"You look nice today," Helen Anne said, smiling. She tapped her security fob to the scanner and pressed the number three.

"Thank you." He smoothed a few wrinkles from his pants and then added, "These are my lucky shoes. Did I ever tell you about how I closed a fifty-million-dollar deal while wearing these shoes?" He laughed heartily.

He'd told the story many times, but she didn't stop him when he launched into a detailed description of the deal and its repercussions. His long-term memory seemed to get stronger even as his short-term memory faded. She guessed that was something to hold on to.

"What an amazing story, Dad."

He quieted as the elevator rose, and she got the urge to reach over and grab his hand. She didn't follow through, however. Emotion confused him as much as anything lately, and she didn't want to have to explain herself. She kept both hands folded in front of her and tried not to think of the depressing road they were on. Instead, she could worry about making a fool of herself dancing with Giovanni.

She looked down at her feet and tried to remember the last time she'd done any kind of dancing. Her wedding. Seventeen years ago. God, that was pathetic.

"Where are we going?" her father asked again.

And the explanation started all over.

Once Helen Anne had settled her father in his captive office, which was attached to Rachel's, she slipped into the reception area right outside the door to get the cup of coffee he'd demanded. Sometimes she worried he didn't recognize her, that he spoke gruffly, like she was his secretary, because he thought she was.

Shaking off that thought, she popped a decaf pod into the coffee maker and tapped her fingers on the counter top as she waited for the Aces' embossed mug to fill.

"Morning, Helen Anne!" Adele Packer, Rachel's secretary, set an overstuffed tote and brown-bag lunch on the desk a few feet from Helen Anne.

"Good morning." She lifted the coffee with one hand and reached for a napkin with the other.

Adele disappeared into Rachel's office, and the elevator chimed. More people filled the reception area. Benny Bryant, the Aces' general manager, was dressed in a pinstriped suit and carried a leather briefcase. Beside him, a man Helen Anne recognized but not by name fussed with his phone. "Slater says Caceres is still in the weight room, so I'll catch him later."

The men split and entered their respective offices. So Giovanni was in the weight room? Helen Anne had texted him yesterday and told him to meet her in the empty training room Rachel had offered for dance practices. What if he'd forgotten? He probably had. Typical man. But an unwanted image of him covered in sweat as he lifted weights three floors below her emblazoned on her brain. Fine, he wasn't exactly typical. Still, a hot body and million-dollar smile didn't make up for a lack of judgment and an abundance of immaturity. She had a broken windshield to prove it.

"Is that for Dad?" Rachel sidled up beside her.

Helen Anne blinked at the coffee in her hand. "Oh. Yeah. I … " Rachel's knowing smile unsettled her. "Morning!" Helen Anne went for carefree and sounded a little deranged.

Rachel reached for the coffee. "I'll take that. *You* have some place to be." She hip checked Helen Anne toward the elevators.

"You know, I'm starting to wonder about you." Helen Anne kept her voice low so as not to be overheard. "You're awfully pushy about this for it to be all about me. What's in it for you? Huh?"

Rachel looked wounded. "I told you! When I read his updated bio and saw he could dance, you came to mind. Then when Sam had to back out of coaching, it just made sense to give you a little shove. I don't see how I'm being anything but generous and sisterly."

Helen Anne tilted her head and regarded Rachel with suspicion. "Rach, I know you. You might be generous and sisterly, but there's always something in it for you. I'd just like to know what it is before I make a complete fool out of myself."

Rachel's gaze zipped back and forth over Helen Anne's head as she seemingly mulled things over. "Fine." She glanced over her shoulder toward the empty reception area before she continued. "He's gunning for a minor league contract, and I can't afford to lose him. Not yet. I'm trying to win a championship, and I need my best players on the field. If I get him involved around town and outside this team, then maybe it won't hurt so much when I make the decision for him."

Helen Anne gaped.

"Don't look at me like that," Rachel said. "It's part of the business. He's under contract. The decision to let him go is totally up to my business team and me. He puts asses in those seats. *Wins* put asses in those seats. Besides, nobody has come asking about him yet, so save your judgment."

"I might not understand the business of baseball, but you're crazy if you think coaching my daughter and dancing with me is going to be an acceptable consolation prize for a guy like that." She laughed.

"It's only a small part of my plan," Rachel said.

"I don't like it. It sounds like you're sabotaging his career."

"Of course not! I'm just slowing down his trajectory. If he helps me get a championship out of this season, then I'll sign off on whatever he wants next season."

"You're evil."

"I prefer evil genius. Now, get the heck out of here and go do my bidding."

Unfortunately, the bidding would have to wait, because Giovanni wasn't in the training room like he was supposed to be. Helen Anne texted him—three times—and when he didn't answer, she stalked to the weight room to peek through the rectangular window, where several guys where working out. She recognized most of them by their faces. But the guy with his back to her, the guy with a complicated maze of muscles rippling and flexing beneath his bare, bronze skin—she recognized him by something else, something that fluttered in her stomach and stuttered in her breath. *Sweet Jesus.*

"Helen Anne?"

Her heart skipped a beat as she turned to face the statuesque African-American woman standing behind her.

Pauly Byrne, the Aces' pitcher and only female playing in the Independence League, wore a workout bra, basketball shorts, and a genuine smile. "How are you? It's good to see you again."

They'd been in shared company a few times over the last two years, and every time Helen Anne struggled to reconcile this model-caliber beauty with the take-no-prisoners beast who took the mound. "It's good to see you too. Are you excited for the season?"

"Pumped," Pauly said, and then she glanced behind Helen Anne to the weight room. "Were you waiting for someone? Is Sam in there?" But then she noticed Helen Anne's yoga pants, Aces' T-shirt, and running shoes, and her smile broadened. "Or are you here to work out?"

"No. I, uh, well, I'm actually … I need to talk to Giovanni Caceres," she said. "He's supposed to be dancing with me in a school fundraiser."

"That's awesome!" Pauly reached behind Helen Anne and pulled open the door, before Helen Anne had the good sense to stop her. "Gio, you have a visitor."

Pulsing music filtered into the hallway, and way too many pairs of eyes flashed in Helen Anne's direction, including Giovanni's. His blank face clouded the minute he saw her.

Great.

"Thank you." Helen stepped aside so Pauly could enter the gym, and when she did, Giovanni exited. Without his shirt.

The flutters in her stomach rose to the base of her throat, but they were balanced out by an annoyance building in her head. She had exactly one hour to devote to dancing before she needed to head home, shower, and be at the bookstore for a shift change. "You forgot, didn't you?"

He was clean-shaven like he'd been the other day, tan without effort, and his lips were perfectly shaped and pleasantly pink. His coppery brown eyes crinkled as he smiled, and she gave in to impulse, stealing a peek at his chest. Chiseled, defined, and glistening with sweat. *Yowza.*

"What can I say?" His smile turned arrogant with the knowledge she'd been checking him out. "I was really into my workout."

Wait a minute. Did he just pulse his pecs? *Ick.*

Helen Anne steeled her gaze. "I know between my sister and the windshield, you've been cornered into dancing with me, but this fundraiser is important to a lot of people, especially the kids, a lot of whom look up to you. If you can't be serious about helping someone other than yourself, then forget about it. I'll find somebody better." She turned to leave.

"Wait." His brusque voice stopped her mid-step. "There's no way in hell you're going to find somebody better than me." He snorted. "Let me grab my shirt, and I'll meet you in the training room."

Typical jock. No, typical *man*. She could only hope, one of these days, his arrogance would be his undoing.

• • •

It wasn't bad enough to be hounded by one Reed woman, Giovanni had to be hounded by two.

In his defense, when Helen Anne had texted the other day about rehearsing, he'd been half asleep, trying to recover from a hangover. But like hell would he admit to that and risk word getting back to Rachel.

"Do you know how to waltz?" Helen Anne deadpanned.

A waltz? This was going to be more painful than he'd thought. "We won't kick anyone's ass with a waltz."

"I don't want to kick anyone's … " She made a face that said his word choice was beneath her, "butt."

Frustration boiled up inside of him. "Then why are you wasting your time—and mine?"

She blinked a few times but recovered with her snootiness intact. "Because winning isn't everything." He opened his mouth to rebut, but she stole his comeback. "And don't say it's the only thing. That's a very narrow-minded, immature way of viewing the world."

Was she for real? Holy annoying and uptight! Even dressed in loose-fitting clothes. That Aces' T-shirt hid most of the curves he'd admired outside the cages the other day, but he could still make out the swell of her breasts. How 'bout he made those his narrow-minded focus? Tossed around a few suggestive comments. She would lose her shit.

Still, as much as he would love to annoy her as much as she was annoying him, he didn't care to see the inside of Rachel's office—again.

He shrugged his painful resignation. "Whatever." He wasn't willing to risk his baseball career for this woman and some middle school dance.

"Good. Then I say we waltz. I waltzed at my wedding. It was very elegant."

She said elegant, and he heard "stuffy." She said wedding and he pitied the poor dude. Were they still married?

"What do you have against elegance?" she asked.

"It's boring."

To his surprise, her haughty expression crumbled. "Oh. Well, I don't want to be boring."

"Then how 'bout you tell me what you want to be, and I'll pick the dance that fits."

Her shoulders drooped. "I don't know. I guess I want to be … " She folded her arms across her chest for a few seconds and stared off into space. Then she propped her fists on her hips and looked at the floor. "I don't know. I … I just want to be something other than poor Helen Anne whose husband left her. I just want to make my daughter proud."

Well, that was more than he'd expected to learn about her. He chewed on the extraneous information for a few seconds, while she regarded him with uncertainty in her eyes.

"Is there a dance for that?" she asked.

He laughed. "Yeah. I know a few that'll work." He slipped his phone from his pocket and searched through the music. "But this one will bring down the house. I'll play the song once so you can get a feel for the pace, and then I'll break it down without the music to teach you the basic steps."

He propped his phone on a waist-high pile of yoga mats in the corner of the room as the lively song began with words shouted in Spanish. A second later, horns blared. When he turned back around, her eyes were wide.

"What is this?"

"Salsa, and it's never boring." He flashed a wolfish grin and placed a hand on the elastic of his shorts, rolling his hips to the ricky-ticky rhythm.

"Oh, I don't think so." She stood there, perfectly still, back straight, while she watched him move. "I can't do that."

"Sure you can." He stepped toward her. "We'll go slow."

"Really … " She jumped backward when he reached for her. "I can't. I won't. I'm fine with being boring now that I think about it."

Well, too bad for her he didn't play it safe, especially not on the dance floor. If she was dancing with him, neither would she.

The music died, and Giovanni studied her worried expression. "Think of it this way. If we salsa, nobody's going to be thinking about your ex-husband. And your daughter? She's gonna think you're a beast."

Helen Anne cracked a small smile. "A beast, huh? I don't know about that. That's a stretch."

"You won't know unless you try."

A few more seconds ticked by as she gnawed her bottom lip, and then she nodded. "Okay. Teach me."

"Excellent." Mostly because teaching her a routine he already knew would save him precious time. "Since we have a short rehearsal today, I'll just show you the core steps." Her brows raised, and her superior expression said the lack of time was his fault. She still annoyed the crap out of him, but he ignored it and forged ahead. "This is called On1 timing. That just means we'll be stepping forward on Count One."

Her arms and neck were so stiff she looked like a linebacker in full pads. He reached out and grabbed her hand to shake her loose. Tiny, heated prickles licked at his palm.

He dropped her hand. "Relax," he said, his tone unintentionally clipped. "Loosen up."

She gave her limbs an awkward wiggle and managed to settle her arms at her sides.

"Better," he said. "Now, start in a neutral position with your feet together like this."

She slammed her heels together without an ounce of air between them.

Teaching this woman to salsa might take him all damn season.

He touched the heel of his left sneaker to the tips of hers. "Relax," he said again. "Leave some space."

She shimmied her feet apart until there were a few inches of space in between. "Like this?"

When she glanced up, the vulnerability in her eyes surprised him. The lack of confidence didn't seem to mesh with her earlier snobbiness.

"Yep. Like that." He gave her a reassuring smile, because as much as he didn't want to be here right now, getting along with her would make this process a lot easier. And maybe—just maybe—she would pick up the dance quicker, letting him off the practice hook earlier. He patted his left thigh. "Now, we're going to step forward with our left foot like this, and that's Count One."

She copied him.

"Good," he said.

"Kind of hard to mess that up."

He chuckled at her self-deprecation. "You would be surprised." Then he tapped his right thigh. "Next, we're going to step in place with our right foot for Count Two, and then bring back our left foot to the neutral position for Count Three. Count Four is a pause, so we stay here. Got it?"

Her forehead wrinkled with concentration. "Up for one. Lift for two. Back for three. Pause for four." She repeated the words as she performed the steps, and she stood a little straighter when she got them right.

"Perfect," he said, feeling hopeful she was catching on. "Now, we're going to perform the same sequence in reverse, stepping back with the right foot first."

They went through those steps a few times with Giovanni counting 1, 2, 3, 4, 5, 6, 7, 8.

"Maybe I *can* do this." There was a brightness in her voice.

"Of course you can." But now, was the moment of truth. Giovanni faced her. "We're going to put it together." He hesitated before he reached behind her with his right hand and flattened his palm against her upper back. No prickles this time, but she was soft and warm through her T-shirt. She was antsy, too. He took her left hand in his, and tried another reassuring smile. "The only difference now is that you're going to start going backward, because I'm leading. Okay? All the steps are the same, though."

"Backward. Got it." She exhaled loudly, but her body stiffened.

He didn't bother correcting her. "Ready? And ... " He pushed against her left hand, "step."

She jerked and tramped on his foot.

"Crud," she said, looking between their bodies. "I was supposed to go backward. I knew that. I don't know what I was thinking."

"Don't worry about it. Missteps are normal when you're learning. We'll go again and again until you get the hang of it."

A few minutes later, they were moving in sync to his counting. Her face was flushed, and her eyes sparkled when she asked, "Who knew six little steps could be so hard?" But doubt flashed across her face again. "I'm guessing there's a lot more to learn unless we want to be the most basic couple out there."

He laughed. "Of course. There's nothing basic about me."

Her lips quirked as she shook her head. "If I could have one tenth of your confidence, I'd be golden."

Without thought, he tightened his arm around her waist as if she were just a woman he'd met in a bar. "You never know. Maybe some of it'll rub off on you."

She shot out of his arms with a haughty laugh. "Yes, well, not today." Then she tapped her watchless wrist. "Time's up."

Yeah, grabbing her like that hadn't been his smartest move.

She backed toward the door. Maybe she was late for her manicure. "I could probably fit in another practice later this week," she said, sounding rushed and nervous. "Same time same place?"

"I guess." But he had to fit in a hitting lesson with Macy, too, on top of his mandated team workouts and practices, and the independent workouts he knew would take him to the next level. Not to mention an exhibition game that would set the tone for this season.

She lifted her chin and narrowed her eyes like she was oh so much more mature and respectable than him. "That doesn't sound too reassuring. Do you think you can remember to be here next time?"

Well, if she was going to be like that, he wasn't sure. He might show up late just to piss her off.

"I don't need to remember," he said flippantly. "If I forget, you'll track me down."

Wasn't that a depressing thought?

Chapter Three

After a quick shower and change, Helen Anne raced to the used bookstore she owned on Main Street to relieve Patrice, the only employee she could afford. The top page of a legal pad she and Patrice used to keep each other up to date after a closing or shift change was covered in Patrice's loopy handwriting. Helen Anne spun the pad around and started reading. *Fifty dollars in sales.* Her stomach rolled, and the ever-present knots tightened with worry.

With a sigh, she temporarily lost herself alphabetizing the children's section. Sitting cross-legged on a nursery-rhyme-themed rug, she flipped through a copy of *Where the Wild Things Are*, and tried not to think about her unsettling reaction to Giovanni when he'd pulled her closer.

Maybe some of it'll rub off on you. Dear God, there was an inappropriate thought. Seriously, what was wrong with her for even stooping to his level and going there?

The bell above the front door rang, and she returned the book to the shelf so she could greet her customer.

Rachel walked in, dressed in her business suit and carrying two to-go cups of coffee. "Dad is home safely, and I had a little time to kill. How did it go?"

"Shouldn't you be checking in on your future father-in-law, the one who just got out of the hospital, instead of checking up on me?"

Rachel shrugged. "Paul is fine. He just needs to listen to the doctor and take it easy. He also needs to listen to me when I say turkey bacon and chicken sausage taste as good as the real thing. You, on the other hand," she held out a cup of coffee, "are still at considerable risk."

Helen Anne accepted the coffee and let it warm up her ice-cold hands. "Considerable risk of what? And for the record, they absolutely do not taste as good as the real thing."

Rachel's eyes widened. "Don't you dare say that to Paul." But her lips curved. "I'm serious, Helen Anne. You're letting this divorce define you. It's been three years, and you haven't been on a single date. I've been here two years, and I haven't seen you have any unbridled fun. You're either holed up in this bookstore or shut in with Mom and Dad at home."

"That's not true. I'm at the school a lot, too."

"Right. Because PTA constitutes unbridled fun."

"It has its moments."

Rachel rolled her eyes. "Only if you're sniffing markers and glue sticks. Seriously. How did the rehearsal go?"

"It was short." She clammed up and second-guessed the wisdom of telling Rachel Giovanni had forgotten. She had no reason to protect him, but she didn't exactly like the idea of Rachel lording over him and using her and her daughter to do it. "I needed to get here so Patrice could leave."

"Did he behave himself?"

She thought of the split-second melding of their bodies and his words: *Maybe some of it will rub off on you.* "Yes. He was the perfect gentleman."

"Now I know you're lying. Giovanni is talented, smooth, and charming. But gentlemanly?" She laughed. "I was hoping some of your refinement and common sense would rub off on him."

Helen Anne choked on hot coffee. Enough already with the rubbing off!

"What did I say?" Rachel asked innocently.

"Nothing. You're just so calculating it's scary. And it makes me a little leery to keep participating in whatever this is."

"I told you what this is. This is you getting a dance partner, and Macy getting a baseball coach, and Dad getting a championship. I don't see how any of that is bad."

"Giovanni might see it differently."

"But he won't, because nobody's going to ask his opinion on it, right? Just trust me. This is the best thing for everybody. Giovanni too. He needs to learn a few hard lessons before he can make it to the majors and actually stay there. Why do you think the Mets let him go?" She raised her brows. "I'll give you one hint. It wasn't just his abysmal batting average and error percentage."

"He was in the majors? Really? What happened?"

"The usual. Too much partying and too many women. It's what happens when you take a guy who's had a one-track, baseball-oriented mind and give him what he's always wanted. He thinks he's finally made it, so he backs off a bit and ends up with too much free time."

Not that it didn't make sense, considering Helen Anne had pegged Giovanni as being immature from the beginning, but she wondered, "When did you get to be such an expert on professional athlete psychology?"

"When I bought a team full of guys with inferiority complexes, the love of my life included." Rachel grinned. "You are actually doing Giovanni a huge favor by being a pillar of stability in his life."

Helen Anne swallowed a harsh laugh. "So I'm his mother figure."

"Whatever works."

Not that. That just made her feel a lot older than thirty-six. And what if everybody else in town thought the same thing when she and Giovanni took the stage? He was what? Twenty-five? On the bright side, at least they wouldn't be thinking about Jeremy leaving her.

In the distance, her phone rattled against the countertop, where she kept it tucked beside the register.

"Let me make sure that's not Macy," she said.

Rachel followed her to the counter. "How's she doing with baseball?"

"Fine I guess. She doesn't tell me much. She ... " The name Jeremy Gardner flashed across Helen Anne's phone screen. "Crap. What does he want?"

"Who?"

Helen Anne flashed the phone at Rachel.

"Answer it," Rachel said. "I'm here for backup."

Helen Anne took a deep breath and answered. These days, Jeremy never called unless it was important. "Hello."

Rachel moved closer.

"I have some news." He sounded good. Chipper. Which Helen Anne welcomed, because whatever was good for him was good for Macy ... usually.

"What news?" She tilted the phone away from her ear as Rachel leaned in.

"Vikki and I are getting married."

Rachel covered her mouth, and Helen Anne backed against the counter for support. She wasn't surprised Jeremy was moving on so definitively after the divorce, but she was surprised a grown woman would fall for his antics. She'd been eighteen. She had an excuse.

"Congratulations?" Vikki seemed like a decent person, and once even, Helen Anne had tried to tactfully warn her away from the man who had stolen Helen Anne's best years.

"I don't want or need your blessing," Jeremy said. "This call is purely informational. The engagement announcement is running in the Arlington *Sentinel* tomorrow."

Of course it was. Never mind that Jeremy and Vikki didn't even live in Arlington. This was a typical selfish, exhibitionist move meant to humiliate her. Classic Jeremy.

Rachel reached for the phone, and Helen Anne stepped away.

"Are you going to call Macy?" she asked. "Don't you think she should hear about this from you instead of from the paper?"

"What twelve-year-old reads the newspaper? You can tell her."

She wanted so badly to say, "Tell her yourself," but the instinct to shield Macy from Jeremy's particular brand of cruelty was too strong. "Fine."

"I'm taking Vikki on a trip to celebrate. Tell Macy I'll buy her something while I'm away."

"How nice of you." Helen Anne laced her words with more sarcasm than she knew she had. But the minute the loaded words left her mouth, she cowered.

"Look at you. Growing a backbone." His laugh wasn't friendly. "Be careful. You don't want to shoot for bold and end up bitchy. It's not attractive at your age. I mean what would people think?"

Oh, he knew exactly what people would think. *Poor Helen Anne. Alone and unhappy.* That's why he was running the engagement announcement in the Arlington *Sentinel*. To highlight how far he'd come since the divorce—and how far she'd fallen.

"He's just trying to rattle you," Rachel said after the call had ended.

"Well, he succeeded. He's getting married. He's happy. He's living an exciting life in the city. And I'm still here, doing the same damn things, living with my mom and dad."

"There's more to it than that. There's more to you. And dancing with Giovanni is something different. What better way to face them all—Jeremy included—than by taking that stage and making your own announcement?"

Maybe. But Helen Anne still had some pride left. And every ounce of it questioned if salsa dancing with a man ten years her junior was the statement she wanted to make.

•••

Giovanni kept his limbs loose and his eyes on the batter. In his peripheral vision, he could see his teammates spread out over the entire field. He'd always loved the vantage point from center field.

After months of practicing, it felt good to get out here and face another team. It felt even better to be up by two in the bottom of the sixth against the Dayton Bulldogs, who Coach Slater had described as arguably their biggest obstacle to a championship. Not that Giovanni intended to be around long enough to win that championship. But performing well against a top-rated team would get him noticed by a minor-league scout much faster.

Pauly delivered a fastball down the pipe, and the batter cranked the ball up and over right field.

Giovanni shifted, keeping his eyes on the rising speck as he sprinted toward right field. The ball had the height for a homer, but dragged in the hearty breeze.

Right fielder Lenny Craig ran too deep but caught his mistake and corrected. At the last possible second, he dove for the ball, which bounced off the tip of his glove and rolled by him.

Meanwhile, the batter rounded the bases and ended with a stand-up triple.

Giovanni hated two-out rallies. This was exactly why you didn't start packing up your bat bag until all nine innings had been played.

He reset and focused on the next batter.

Pauly's next pitch hit the dirt in front of Reece and got away from him for a second, long enough for the runner on third to break for the plate. But Reece was quick, and the runner retreated.

Come on, Pauly. Hold it together for one more out.

The ball left her hand and a moment later soared above second base. The wind pushed hard against Giovanni's back as he sprinted toward the spot where he expected the ball to land. Another gust and the ball landed short. He ran hard; getting there a split-second after the ball hit the ground. He still had time to gun the guy out.

Giovanni locked his eyes on Reece, who was in position at the plate. He put everything he had into that throw, visualizing the ball as a missile on a course with destiny.

The ball reached Reece along with the runner, and the collision rattled the air. Both men sprawled across the baseline. All at once, shocked silence descended on the field, and time seemed to still. Nobody moved.

Fuck.

Cries of agony prompted a flurry of activity from the dugouts.

Giovanni jogged toward second base.

The runner was helped to his feet by his coach and trainer, which left Reece writhing at home plate.

"Shit. That doesn't look good," second baseman Roy Willet said.

It looked even worse when an ambulance drove onto the field.

Giovanni dropped to one knee. He'd been through a lot with Reece, who had also been his roommate these last two years, but nothing compared to seeing the guy like this.

"What the fuck was wrong with that guy?" Hank Carlyle, the shortstop, joined them. "He went out of his way to take out Reece. I had a clear view of the plate. Reece wasn't blocking it."

"It was my throw," Giovanni said, solemnly.

"No, man," Hank said. "That throw was right on. The runner was a dick, and I'm going to make sure Pauly knows it."

After a short stint in the dugout, where the trainer informed everyone that Reece more than likely had a dislocated knee, the Aces' were back on the field.

"Dislocated knee doesn't sound too bad," Leftfielder Dante Regis said as he ran beside Giovanni to the outfield.

Giovanni shook his head in disbelief. "How long have you been playing this game? Best case scenario, he's done for the season. Worst case, he's done for good."

Through three batters, those deplorable options rolled through Giovanni's head, making his blood boil.

Finally, with two outs and a man on second, the son of a bitch who'd taken Reece out stepped up to the plate.

It was time for a little retribution. Everybody on the field and in the Aces' dugout knew it.

Pauly drilled one right at the guy's head.

Everything happened so fast. The guy hit the dirt, and the rest of his team rushed the field to defend him. The Aces followed, Giovanni included. He sprinted toward the mound, where a swarm of ball players gathered in a massive shoving match with Pauly in the middle.

The coaching staffs from both teams picked guys off the outer edge of the violent circle, but Giovanni avoided them. He wanted to protect his pitcher, but then he caught sight of the dick who'd ended his roommate's season. The guy was about to escape the scuffle without so much as a scratch on his face. That didn't sit right with Giovanni, so he cocked his arm and said, "This is for Reece" right before his fist crushed the guy's nose.

A second later, he was being strangled by his jersey gone taut around his neck as Coach Slater pulled him off the field.

"Dumbass!" Coach growled the word. "Clean up your shit and head to the locker room."

There was no doubt once the umpires got a handle on the fighting Giovanni would be thrown out of this exhibition game. The question was would he be suspended for Opening Day.

The answer was waiting for him in the locker room in the form of Rachel Reed.

She stood with her arms crossed and her eyes sharp. "When are you going to learn to keep your nose clean?"

When there was nobody left to defend, he guessed, but he kept his mouth shut and faced the music.

Chapter Four

Giovanni avoided a league-issued suspension, because the incident had been during an exhibition game and so many other players had been involved. Along with him, Pauly and Ian had been ejected and were now subject to team-issued punishment.

Boy, did misery ever love company—especially when the miserable were banished from the practice field and cleaning the locker room toilets instead.

"I will never know how you guys can have such bad aim." Pauly brushed hair out of her eyes with the back of her rubber-gloved hand. "It's the same way at home—everything covered in piss and hair thanks to my brothers."

"Yeah, because you're so innocent," Ian snapped.

"If that's a knock on me pegging the batter in return for him laming Reece, I happily accept the consequences."

"No, it's a knock on you pitching like shit in the first place, which put us all in that situation."

Pauly flipped him off.

Giovanni threw his sponge into the bucket and stripped off his gloves. "Stop! You guys are acting like a bunch of victims. Reece is the one who's never going to play ball again. Imagine how he fucking feels?"

As bad as it was being cut from the Mets then having to swallow his pride and try out for an indie-pro team where the owner breathed down his neck, at least Giovanni was still physically able to play baseball.

Pauly sat back on her heels. "I can't believe the sprain was that bad. I mean, when it happened, it didn't look like a season-ending injury."

Ian hopped up from his crouch with the natural grace of a catcher who was about to be seeing a lot more playing time. "I gotta get some air."

When he'd gone, Pauly went back to cleaning. "I doubt we'll see him again."

Knowing Ian, she was probably right, and as much as Giovanni craved his freedom too, he couldn't risk getting caught abandoning his post. He reached for his rubber gloves but stopped when a phone vibrated on the metal shelf that ran beneath the mirrors.

"Yours or mine?" Pauly asked.

He hopped up for a look. "Mine. My mother."

"Answer it. Mothers don't like to wait. And tell her I said hi."

"Will do." But he wasn't going to tell his mother what they were doing and why they were doing it. "*Mamá!*" he said as he stepped out of the bathroom and into the empty locker room. "What's going on?"

"I tell you what's goin' on, *cariño*. I'm in hell. Ju think they'd have a table big enough for sewing, but no. No table." Carlotta swore in Spanish. "No respect for the talent." She even rolled her "r's with melodramatic flair. "I want to see you."

"I know. I want to see you too. We'll figure something out. Maybe after the season."

"No! Too long. Come get me now. Get me out of hell."

"*Mamá!* You're not in hell!" His sister Lucia's voice grew louder until she was talking directly into the phone. "The theater is gorgeous, Gio, and we have private dressing rooms. They give us catered meals after every performance."

"No table!" Carlotta yelled in the background, and Giovanni laughed. He missed them, and after rehearsing with Helen Anne, he missed the dancing a little, too.

"If I had known she was going to try to guilt you into coming to see her, I wouldn't have let her call," Lucia said.

"I don't care. It's good to hear your voices. Where's Rosa?"

Lucia laughed. "Trying to scrounge up a table."

"Giovanni!"

His heart stopped at the sound of his name bellowed from his father's mouth.

"*Papá*, don't yell like that," Lucia said. "You're gonna wake the dead."

"Your brother's gonna be dead when I get hold of him. Give me the phone."

"Don't," Giovanni said, but it was too late. The scuffling in the background told him the handoff was happening whether he liked it or not. His only options now were to deal with his father or hang up.

He might be trouble from time to time, but he wasn't disrespectful to his father.

"*Papá!*"

"Don't ju papá me! I read online. I see. Ju been fighting again."

Shit. He hadn't thought about local news selling him out all the way across the country. "The guy deserved it."

"*¡Tienes que aprender a controlarte!*"

"I *am* controlling myself." Most of the time.

Giovanni listened as his father chastised him some more in Spanish. It would've gone on a lot longer if Coach Slater hadn't walked into the locker room.

"*Papá*, Coach is here. I gotta go."

Coach Slater raised his brows and pointed to the bathroom. Giovanni started walking without saying a word.

"Where's Pratt?" Coach asked when they met up with Pauly.

"Using another bathroom," she said without flinching.

Coach accepted the excuse with a nod. "Return this crap to the maintenance closet and get your asses to the weight room to make up for the missed practice. Got it?"

"Yes, sir," Pauly said, hopping to her feet.

Giovanni breathed a sigh of relief.

"Caceres," Coach added. "You're wanted upstairs first."

Of course he was. First his father ripped him a new one. Now the team owner wanted her turn. What a bang-up day.

When he reached Rachel's office she gestured to the leather chairs in front of her desk. "Sit," she said.

A light sheen covered his palms, but he kept his breathing in check. He'd defended himself as best he could following the incident, and she'd seemed disappointed but reasonably calm. Maybe now that she'd had time to think about it, she'd decided he hadn't been punished enough. Worse case, she cut him from the team.

"I'm sorry," he said, rising off the chair an inch or two.

"You said that already, and I believe you. I also believe that as sorry as you are, this impulsivity is a pattern you can't seem to break." She pinned him in place with an icy glare. "You were the only player to throw a punch."

More like he was the only player who landed a punch. But that probably wasn't his best defense now.

He settled in the chair again, his fingers digging into his thighs. "It was one time. I haven't been in another physical altercation since I came to Arlington."

"Well then it's extra-sad you fell off the wagon, and it's all the more reason for me to insist on some stability in your life. Coach Slater told me you need to find a host family now that Reece is gone."

This oughta be good. How much did he want to bet she found some straitlaced preacher, who would insist on Bible study every morning?

"I can manage," he said. "I might be able to squeeze in with Pratt and Carlyle."

Rachel laughed. "I don't think so. I'm trying to save you from flushing your career down the toilet."

"In that case, thanks, because I've had enough of toilets for one day."

The crack about his punishment seemed to be lost on her as she shuffled around in her top drawer. She withdrew a white business envelope and pushed it toward him. "I've arranged for you to live in a fully furnished, two-bedroom, two-bath carriage house. There's also a Jeep Wrangler at your disposal. The address is in this envelope along with the code to open the door. The keys to the Jeep are in the glove box."

He stared at the envelope locked beneath her hand and held his breath. What was the catch? "I thought you said I would be with a host family."

"You will be. My family, which makes it much easier for me to keep an eye on you." She flashed a lethal smile.

He'd heard of team owners going to extremes to protect their assets, but this was crazy. "With all due respect … "

"Giovanni, we need each other. Period. Your preseason has been electric—minus the brawl. You're playing better than I've ever seen you play, which has me thinking a championship is in reach. I want to hoist that trophy and hand it to my dad as much as you want another shot at the MLB. Last year, fourteen guys in the Independence League had their contracts purchased by minor league teams. This year, you could be one of them. On talent alone, you *should* be one of them. But you have to demonstrate some growth and maturity on and off the field."

He resisted the urge to scowl, because a small part of him worried she was right.

Rachel pushed the envelope closer. "Take it."

Again, she had him cornered.

Giovanni reluctantly accepted and ground out a "thank you."

He couldn't handle much more of this. One way or another, he was going to play his way out of Arlington and prove he wasn't the loser everybody thought he was.

• • •

On Thursday, Jeremy's beady-eyed engagement photo and the accompanying announcement appeared on the front page of the Lifestyle section. One look at the smiling couple, who was said to be planning a destination wedding in Aruba, and Helen Anne had wanted to pull the covers over her head and stay in bed. But that would've meant rescheduling the fundraising committee's monthly meeting, and that would've made her look guilty as sin. Cue the pity.

Helen Anne edged between the chattering women gathered around her kitchen table to serve glasses of freshly squeezed lemonade.

"Every time I come here, I feel like I'm visiting Martha Stewart." Candace Wall gave a wistful look around the Reeds' eat-in, French-country-inspired kitchen. "You're so lucky, Helen Anne. If my parents had a house like this, I would never move out either."

Across the table, Mertz Pullman and Katie Ring exchanged quick glances. Helen Anne could imagine what they were thinking, but so far no one had actually brought up the topic of Jeremy's engagement. Was it possible they hadn't seen it? Was it possible they didn't care?

"Thank you, Candace." Helen Anne traded the pitcher of lemonade for a platter of frosted pinwheel cookies. Then she made her way back to the table, where she took a seat beside Laura Kuhl.

The room grew uncomfortably quiet, and all eyes shifted to her.

"Do you want to talk about it?" Mertz asked, her bushy brows pulling together with concern.

Helen Anne feigned ignorance. "Talk about what?"

"Oh, honey." Laura reached beneath the table and grabbed Helen Anne's hand.

Her back went rigid, and her heart lodged in her throat. She gracefully wiggled her hand free and glanced around the table at four women she would call friendly but not exactly friends. "If this is about Jeremy's engagement, there's no need for pity. I'm happy for him. For them. What's good for Jeremy is good for Macy. And me. I'm in a good place. We're all in a good place. I don't need your pity."

Laura reached behind her and patted and rubbed her back.

Frustration welled up in the form of tears Helen Anne refused to shed. She was not sad about losing Jeremy; she was upset half this town thought she should be.

"Now, about the fundraiser," she said, briskly.

"How's your father?" Katie asked.

Helen Anne swallowed a groan with a gulp of lemonade. Before she could launch another defense against their pity, Candace asked, "For the love of God, who is that?"

Candace, Katie, and Mertz all left their chairs and pressed themselves against the picture windows overlooking the carriage house, the swimming pool, and the bucolic backyard. Helen Anne's view was blocked by their bodies.

"I don't know," she said. "Maybe some landscaper."

"He's with your sister," Mertz said.

"Then it's Sam." Helen Anne leaned to the right and tried to see around Katie.

"He's not Sam," Mertz said. "This guy's dark. Maybe Mexican."

Helen Anne shot out of her seat. According to his bio, Giovanni was Venezuelan.

"He's hot, whoever he is," Candace said.

He was the last thing Helen Anne wanted to deal with right now. What the heck would he be doing at her house with Rachel anyway?

"Ladies, if you'll excuse me, I'll go make sure my sister doesn't interrupt us."

"But he can!" Candace said, and the rest of them laughed.

Helen Anne stepped out of the house, buzzing with annoyance, and called to her sister. Rachel and Giovanni's heads turned simultaneously. His face wrinkled, and he looked confused to see her. How was that for irony?

"What are you guys doing here?" Helen Anne asked.

"I'm showing him around the carriage house." Rachel spoke the words like they were completely reasonable.

Helen Anne pursed her lips and glanced at Giovanni. He wore track pants and a faded Coastal Carolina T-shirt that spread across his muscular chest like a velvety-soft second skin. And he looked about as happy to be here as she was to have him.

"Why?" Helen Anne asked.

"He needs a place to live, and we have more than enough room."

The ground shifted beneath Helen Anne's feet a second before he asked, "You live here?"

She blinked. "I do."

"Think of how convenient this will be for dance rehearsals," Rachel said, brightly, but Helen Anne knew it was just a cover for more conniving. "And you'll have all this wide open space to help Macy with baseball."

Giovanni's expression hardened, but whatever he was thinking he kept to himself.

Helen Anne didn't want to feel bad for him, but she did. Rachel had gone too far.

"We really need to talk about this, but I'm busy." Helen Anne pointed to the kitchen window.

Rachel waved in their direction, and when Helen Anne turned, she saw the women were aiming their deranged smiles at Giovanni. Candace literally had her body pressed against the glass.

"Do *they* live here?" His voice was cool, but there was a hint of humor.

She couldn't help herself; she chuckled. "God, no. It's bad enough hosting them for the occasional PTA meeting."

By the time Helen Anne returned to the kitchen, Stacy had arrived. She was the only woman not crowded around the window.

"Why didn't you tell us he's your dance partner?" Katie asked.

"Because she wants to keep him all to herself," Mertz said.

Helen Anne shook her head wildly. "That's not … "

"No wonder you said you didn't want anybody's pity." Candace bobbed her penciled-on brows.

"It's not like that," Helen Anne said over their excited chatter.

With a noisy exhale and both hands over her heart, Laura seemed relieved. "He looks old enough to be my kid."

Oh, please! But Helen Anne's neck heated as she did the math in her head. Giovanni's bio said he was twenty-five. Eleven years difference. *Ha!* Laura might be old enough to be his mother, but Helen Anne wasn't.

In the chaos, Stacy reached for a cookie and smiled sheepishly at Helen Anne. "I'm sorry. I thought they knew."

"Wait!" Katie's nose was pressed to the glass. "Why is your sister leaving him in your garage?"

Helen Anne grabbed a few cookies amid a labored sigh. "He's not in the garage. He's in the carriage house." All eyes turned on her. "He lives there."

A brief silence fell and she swallowed hard, just waiting to hear their opinions on that bit of news.

"Damn," Candace finally said, reverently. "You weren't kidding when you said you were in a good place."

Chapter Five

Helen Anne closed the bookstore door behind her, but didn't rush to turn over the open sign. This was her only Giovanni-free zone. Even her PTA meetings at school had become a haven for side-eyed glances and suggestive smiles—no matter how many times she denied the ridiculous idea that she was doing anything other than dancing with the man.

She moved silently over the rust-colored area rug that led from the door to the checkout counter, past rows of antique wooden shelving, and set her travel mug and mobile phone beside the vintage register. The legal pad read, *Thirty dollars.* Helen Anne winced. Friday nights were traditionally slow, but thirty dollars was abysmal. She had enough in savings and from the divorce settlement to keep the doors open for about six months, maybe nine if she cut back on new orders. But beyond that? Something big needed to happen to keep this place afloat.

Lost in mental financial calculations, Helen Anne reached for her coffee and suddenly heard a high-pitched hiss. She froze, narrowing in on the sound, trying to place its direction. It was coming from the back of the store.

Helen Anne followed the hissing to the storeroom, where she flipped on the lights and saw fine streams of water shooting violently from an elbow-shaped pipe in the corner of the unfinished ceiling.

"No, no, no, no, no, no, no!" This was *not* the something big she had in mind.

Puddles formed on the weathered, original hardwood floors and crept beneath the stacks of boxes filled with books she'd recently purchased from a library sale.

With a yelp of helplessness, she scrambled down the dark hallway to the back exit and reached above the door to crank the shut off valve.

After she called her landlord, who assured he was on his way, she left a message for her local insurance agent, and then she glanced at the wall clock. Macy would be done with her hitting lesson in about an hour. Helen Anne couldn't exactly run out to pick her up and bring her back to the store like she'd planned to. Her default support was Rachel, but Rachel had agreed to take their parents to Pittsburgh for the day to visit extended family.

Now what? She could ask Giovanni to drop Macy off. After all, Macy was with him, and he was driving the Jeep. It seemed like the sensible solution. The drive here from the stadium wasn't long, and Macy was comfortable with the guy. But still, Helen Anne hesitated. She did not want this man involved in their lives any more than he had to be.

When it was clear she was going to spend the better part of the day cleaning up and gathering information about repairs, she gave in and called him.

"Hello." He sounded winded.

"Hi. Is Macy with you?"

"Of course she's with me. She'll be here until you pick her up."

"Right. I know. Listen, I have a favor to ask." Silence thundered on his end of the line. "A pipe burst at my store, and I'm kind of in a big mess here. Could you possibly bring her to me when the lesson is over?"

More silence, the kind that came with desperately trying to figure a way out.

"I wouldn't ask if I had another option, but Rachel and my mom and dad are out of town for the day."

"Okay," he said. It wasn't enough of a response for her to know whether he was really okay with this or not, but she could guess.

"Thank you," she said. "I really appreciate it."

An hour later, as Helen Anne said goodbye to her less-than-helpful landlord, she saw Macy and Giovanni strolling up the sidewalk.

"We put the top down," Macy said, her smile beaming.

Helen Anne hated riding with the top down. Too cold. Too windy. Too exposed. Too dangerous.

She glanced at Giovanni who was wearing his typical cut-off shirt and athletic shorts despite an uncharacteristic chill in the April air. "Please tell me you wore seatbelts."

"Yes, Mom," Giovanni said, flatly, but then the corner of his mouth ticked.

She didn't find it funny. Not one bit. She held open the door for Macy and turned to him, intending to thank him and send him on his way. But he brushed past her ensconced in a cloud of fresh-and-clean man scent, grazing her breast and shoulder with his warm arm.

And just like that, her store was no longer a Giovanni-free zone.

"Is there a lot of damage?" he asked.

She blinked.

"From the pipe?" he added.

"Not enough for my landlord to take it seriously." Her jaw clenched. "He said to call a plumber and a cleanup crew, and we'll square it away later."

Ahead of them, Macy grabbed a book off a shelf and settled into her favorite overstuffed armchair with her legs tucked beneath her.

Giovanni looked similarly relaxed, standing with his feet shoulder width apart and his hands shoved in the pocket of his court shorts. The right hand fiddled with his keys or his change or whatever else was in there … so close to his crotch. He could go now. She would rather not—for any reason—be thinking about his crotch.

"Well then, I'll get out of your way," he said.

That was the best news she'd heard all day.

• • •

While Helen Anne took a phone call, Giovanni said goodbye to Macy and then headed for the door.

"And how much will that cost?" she asked whoever was on the phone.

He made the mistake of glancing back. She leaned against the counter on one elbow, her head propped in her hand, her brow furrowed, and her lips twisted.

"Seriously? Just to come out?" She shifted her hand to cover her eyes and exhaled loudly. "What if I wait until Monday during regular business hours? How much then?"

Why was a woman who drove a Range Rover and lived in a house that looked like a private school worried about money?

It was none of his business. He should leave—get back to the solo workout he was missing—but … he was intrigued. He loitered, glanced at the bindings of a few way-too-thick books, and got the feeling the news on the phone wasn't good.

When she ended the call, he walked over to the counter. "Can I take a look at the damage?"

She wrinkled her nose. He couldn't tell if it was in annoyance or suspicion. "Why?"

"Because I might be able to tell you what's wrong and save you some money."

"Really? So you don't just play ball and dance, you're a plumber now too." Her tone was sarcastic, but there was a light of hope in her brown eyes.

"Not licensed, but in between dance gigs, I worked a lot of odd maintenance jobs with my dad. Every Catholic cathedral we ever worked in had an ancient boiler and leaky pipes, so I have some skill. Not mad skill, but enough to get by."

She seemed to mull that over, gnawing on the inside of her cheek. "Okay. Sure. I mean what can it hurt?"

The leak didn't look like anything major to Giovanni. Nothing that a little plumber's tape and caulk couldn't fix for the time being. It definitely didn't require a weekend service call. Her biggest issue was going to be cleanup, because already the windowless room smelled rank.

Helen Anne was so relieved by his prognosis; she pressed her hands together in prayer formation and squealed.

Curiosity got the better of him, and he set the flashlight she'd given him on a nearby box. "Okay. What gives? You don't strike me as the kind of woman who should be pinching pennies."

Her smile faded. "My divorce was costly and kids are expensive. That doesn't leave a lot for a bookstore."

"Doesn't he pay support?"

She glanced at the empty doorway before she said, "Minimal. He's in sales, and his commissions have been uncharacteristically small lately, so he's had the support amount amended a few times."

"Your folks are like, millionaires, though, right? Couldn't they–"

"My parents bought me the car, because they didn't think the Jeep was a proper 'family' vehicle, and they let me live in their house for free. That's more than generous. The rest is up to me. I won't take a penny from them to help this store."

He could respect that. Giovanni gave Helen Anne a subtle once over. She didn't seem so snobby now. In fact, with random strands of hair falling in front of her eyes and watermarks dotting her wrinkled shirt, he admired her determination.

"I can go to the hardware store and pick up a few things to patch the pipe."

"How much will that cost?"

"Well, if I hide what I need in my hoodie, nothing."

Her eyes widened, and her mouth gaped. The laugh he was expecting never came.

He chuckled to clue her in. "I was kidding. Ten bucks maybe."

"Oh!" A wobbly smile tipped her lips, and she looked relived. "Let me get you some money from the register."

They were a few feet into the main part of the store when Macy jumped in front of them.

"Mom, I'm going to take this book home. Okay?"

The cover featured a black-and-white photo of Lou Gehrig.

"No, Macy. I've told you before that's not okay. These books are for paying customers. You can read whatever you want while you're here, but I don't want you taking anything home. I'm not a library. We have one of those right around the corner."

"But Mom, hardly anybody comes in here. One book won't matter."

Giovanni glanced at Helen Anne in time to see her wounded expression, and he was suddenly torn between this kid who wanted—of all things—a Lou Gehrig bio, and this woman who was surprisingly trying to make ends meet.

Macy hulked away, and Helen Anne continued to the register where she removed a ten-dollar bill from the drawer. "If it ends up being more, I'll pay the difference." She walked around the counter and stopped in front of him.

"It won't." For some unknown reason, he was seriously considering refusing her money and using his own to pay for the materials.

A jingling bell pulled his attention toward the front door, where a curly-headed woman stood.

"Oh my!" She looked right at him when she said it. Then she looked at Helen Anne and raised a fluttering hand to her face. "I, um, I can come back."

Helen Anne did some sort of half-trip, half-jujitsu move to box him out. "Don't be silly, Laura. It's a bookstore. We're open to the public. I mean, today we're technically closed, but you're welcome to come in."

Whoever this Laura was, she peered at him through the lenses of her preppy glasses. "I'm sorry. I didn't know you were closed. The sign says open."

"It must've gotten turned around when someone else came in."

He considered slipping past them both so he could get his hardware run over with and get back to the weight room where he belonged. But Laura kept sneaking peeks at him like he was some deviant who needed to be kept under surveillance.

"I've been busy handling a leaky pipe," Helen Anne said randomly. And as innocent as her words were, they hung in the air like a bad joke.

Giovanni bit back a laugh and turned his head to hide his smile.

"Oh my!" Laura said again, but this time, she took a step backward and reached for the door. "I'll come back another time. Will you be open later?"

"Hopefully," Helen Anne said. "It all depends on how far we get with this pipe."

Did she really not know what she was saying and how it was coming across?

"Yes, of course." Laura left the store with one last glance at him, and Helen Anne flipped the open sign to "closed."

"Why didn't you introduce me?" he asked. "She seemed very interested."

Helen Anne's face was pink when she turned around. "I'm completely mortified."

"Why? I'm the one who should be mortified. It sounded like you were talking about *my* pipe."

Her face went from pink to red. "It did not! *I was not!*" Her gaze flashed behind him. "You know exactly which pipe I was talking about."

"I did, but I don't think she did." He laughed.

Helen Anne covered her face and groaned. "That's just what I need." She threw her hands into the air. "I gave her more ammunition. Half the PTA thinks I'm already ... " She clammed up.

Talk about being intrigued. "They think you're already what?"

"*With* you!" she hissed without really looking at him.

"With me? You mean like ... "

She shushed him and pointed to the back of the store. "I would rather not involve her in this."

"In what?" He grinned. "In our *relationship*?" He wrapped his bedroom voice around the word.

"We aren't having a relationship."

"But they think we are?"

"Yes. Exactly." She waved the ten-dollar bill in his direction. "Now, can we forget all about that and get back to fixing this pipe?"

The whole thing was too damn funny. He glanced down at his groin and then back up at her. "Babe, there ain't nothing wrong with my pipe. For the record."

Helen Anne's cheeks flushed deeper pink but she growled. "Will you just take the money and go?" Frustration laced her words.

He reached for the cash but then withdrew his hand. "What if Laura's hanging around outside, peeking through the window? Won't she think you're paying me for my services?"

Helen Anne checked, craning her neck so she could see up and down the street beyond the picture windows, but then she stopped abruptly and straightened. Looking down at the money in her hand, she smiled like the joke was on him. "Only a man with a broken pipe would charge ten bucks."

It shocked the hell—and a loud laugh—out of him.

"Now, seriously. Take the money." She pushed it toward him, and this time he accepted. "I really am sorry about that. They've been talking crazy ever since they saw you at the house and learned you were my dance partner." She rolled her eyes and added a hint of her trademark haughtiness. "I keep telling them how ridiculous it is—how ridiculous they are—but it goes in one ear and out the other. It's so annoying. And embarrassing!"

What was? The PTA ladies' behavior or the idea of being with him? His ego stewed. Did she think she was too good for him? *Come on.* He'd never met a single woman he couldn't sweet talk in or out of the bedroom. Helen Anne might have a few years on him, but she was no exception to the rule.

He took the money with a smile.

Maybe he would turn up the heat at their next dance rehearsal, just to prove a point.

Chapter Six

At 12:05 p.m. on Saturday, Giovanni walked into the garage beneath the carriage house wearing a pair of shiny black shoes and perfectly tailored slacks. A plain white shirt lay open at his throat, exposing a generous V of velvety brown skin and the curling tips of his chest hair. The air squeezed out of Helen Anne's lungs.

She glanced at her sloppy "Book Worm" T-shirt, gray stretch pants, and apple green running shoes. "You look so nice," she said, a little distressed.

His wide smile crinkled the skin around his sparkling eyes, and she got the unsettling feeling he'd been fishing for that compliment.

Enjoy it, Buddy. Because it wouldn't happen again. Just because he'd patched her pipe and they'd shared a couple laughs didn't mean she was going to let her guard down so they could become chummy and stoke those ridiculous rumors.

"You look nice, too," he said.

He was so full of it. She managed a "yeah, right" look without rolling her eyes. Then she turned her back on him and walked over to the wireless speaker she'd brought out from the house. "I downloaded the song so I could listen to it and practice the steps on my own." She synced her phone with the speaker.

"Good idea." He was behind her now. So close that the heat from his body warmed her back, and the scent of his woodsy cologne filled her head.

She planted a smile on her face and turned around. Mere inches were between them, and she was eye level with the V of his shirt and the swell of his chest.

She obsessively swallowed away the discomfort. "Ready?"

"I was born ready." His grin bordered on predatory.

Something was up. But what? And why?

This time, she rolled her eyes. "That's cheesy, not to mention clichéd."

For a split second the balance of power shifted in her favor as his face blanked, but then a downbeat of lively music sounded, and he reached out, looping an arm around her waist.

His smile came back with a vengeance.

Heat flooded Helen Anne's body, originating from the palms of his hands. She couldn't remember a damn thing. She stepped on his feet a few times. She tripped on her own. She spent the entire song trying to catch up to him.

When the music died, he said, "That was rough." But he was still smiling and holding her hand. "I thought you said you were practicing on your own."

"I have been," she said, wiggling free. "I just wasn't thinking straight."

He raised one genetically sculpted brow. "I wonder why."

But she didn't. Not anymore. He thought he was so smooth. *Gio Suave.* She didn't care if that was cheesy. For some reason, he was trying to mess with her, and she wasn't going to let him.

She frowned. "Let's go again."

This time, she would wipe that confident smile off his face.

She reached behind her to restart the music, and then braced for contact even as she told herself she wouldn't feel anything this time, because there was nothing to feel. She focused on the dance steps instead. *Up for one. Lift for two. Back for three. Pause for four.* And she danced like she had something to prove.

"*¡Excelente!*" he said when the music died a second time.

When he spoke in Spanish, his expression brightened and his voice softened. She liked the effect. In fact, she wouldn't mind hearing him say more.

"Were you born in Venezuela?" she asked, and promptly bit into her cheek while she second-guessed the need to get personal.

"No. I was born in Miami."

"And your parents taught you Spanish. That's so cool. I wish my parents had taught me something about my heritage. All I have is an English coat of arms my father ordered from the Sunday newspaper when I was a kid."

"Well, I was raised in Venezuela by my grandparents until I was five, so they should get the credit for my language skills."

"Oh." She couldn't think of a tactful way to ask why.

His eyes wandered her face in the silence, making her uncomfortable but oddly captivated. "My parents couldn't take care of a baby while they were moving from one dance gig to another, so they left me behind until I was old enough to perform without giving them problems."

"I'm sorry," she said.

He shrugged. "Don't be. I actually wish they'd left me with my grandparents longer."

"You didn't like dancing?"

"Dancing was the only good part." He shoved his hands in his pockets and glanced at his shoes. "Life on the road wasn't easy, because we were always moving. I've lived in hundreds of places in the last twenty years. Maybe thousands."

"Wow." She glanced at the house beyond the driveway and yard and thought about Danny and Jackie, who were probably glued to CNN in the wallpapered family room, waiting for her dance rehearsal to be over so she could tell them all about it. "I've lived in this house my whole life except for the thirteen years I lived with Jeremy. So that makes two places for me."

"Wow," he said, parroting her. "I can't even imagine what that would be like."

"Yeah, you can. It's as boring and predictable as it sounds."

"Boring isn't always bad—or so they tell me." He grinned. "I didn't have much supervision growing up. My sisters and I took care of each other. And they had their work cut out for them." A flash of something dark clouded his face, but then it was like someone pressed the reset button, and he stepped forward with a smile. "Now … " He slipped a hand to her waist and hauled her forward. "Quit stalling." His voice was low and liquid. "Just because you danced it once cleanly doesn't mean you're off the hook. Practice makes perfect."

She wanted to be off the hook—and she didn't. Mostly, she just wanted to stop these confusing feelings that had no basis and no future. But like a mindless robot, she fit her hand to his instead. Strong and warm. She stared into his conflicted eyes and knew there was more to him than she'd expected. But she didn't need and shouldn't want to know how much more.

"Aren't we missing something?" he asked, glancing at their entangled hands.

"What?" Her confusion only deepened when he rubbed his thumb over her knuckle.

"The music." His thumb slid back and forth. "How are you going to turn the music on with your hand way over here?"

"Oh." She watched him tease her knuckle, eliciting tiny tremors in her nerve endings. "That's true." His breath warmed the side of her face, and her stomach tumbled.

What in the world was happening here?

"Helen Anne." The gruff whisper incapacitated her brain, making the only thought in her head, *kiss him*.

"What have we here?"

At the sound of Rachel's voice, they shot apart.

"Hey!" Helen Anne said way too brightly. "What are you doing here?"

"I came to check up on my star player." Rachel's hawk eyes bore into Giovanni, who squirmed. "Was that part of your dance routine or … something else?"

Helen Anne didn't know what to call it, but if the heat in her cheeks was any indication, whatever it was, it wasn't good.

"That was salsa," he said.

"Salsa," Rachel repeated, and her unreadable gaze shifted to Helen Anne. "Maybe Sam and I need to learn to do that. It looks fun."

Helen Anne ignored her growing mortification and stepped between Rachel and Giovanni. "Well, your timing is perfect, because we just finished. Why don't we go in and check on Mom and Dad?"

"Okay," Rachel said, giving Giovanni one last glance.

When they were out of earshot of the garage, Rachel linked her arm with Helen Anne's and said, "That looked cozy."

Helen Anne refused to look at her. "I don't know what you're talking about."

"Oh, come on. I could see the sparks." Rachel tightened her grip. "Bonus! There's nothing like a woman to keep a man around."

Helen Anne stopped short of the house and gaped at her sister. "You're delusional."

"That sparkle in your eyes says I'm not." She grabbed Helen Anne's hands and squeezed. "Just go with it for a little bit. See where it leads. Please. For Dad. For me." She smiled. "But mostly for you. It could be fun."

Or it could backfire spectacularly … like her marriage had. And the last thing Helen Anne wanted was to be starting from the bottom all over again.

•••

After the dance rehearsal, Giovanni couldn't stop thinking about pushing the limits of Helen Anne's self-restraint. Talk about a challenge. Talk about a rush. It could be a hell of a lot of fun. For both of them.

It could also be career suicide. Maybe his impulsivity really was a problem. Rachel already looked at him and saw trouble. He didn't need her thinking he was looking for trouble with her sister. He wasn't.

Well, he hadn't been

He needed a healthy distraction, so he picked up his phone and dialed Ana.

"Surprise, sis," he said when Ana answered. He kept one hand on the Jeep's wheel and headed toward the stadium for evening practice.

"Gio! Oh my God! I miss you."

He hadn't seen her since the off-season, when he'd scrounged up enough to fly to San Diego and crash with his aunt for a couple weeks. "I miss you too. How are the kids?"

"Driving me crazy, just like you used to." Ana didn't dance with the family anymore; she'd become a stay-at-home-mom. "I swear Carlos is going to be the death of me. He got us kicked out of playgroup the other day for knocking the other kids over. Can you believe that? Two years old and he's already headed for juvie."

Giovanni squeezed the steering wheel until his knuckles whitened. "Don't say that. He's way too young to be doing stuff like that on purpose. He's a good kid."

"I know." She paused too long, and Giovanni knew what was coming next.

He wished he'd never made the call.

"You were a good kid too," Ana said. "You just made some bad decisions. But look at you now. How's the season going?"

Whenever she brought up his past transgressions, he felt like he should apologize again. But like he always did, he let her mentions slide. "First regular-season game is next week. We played an exhibition game the other night and it was … " Images of a devastated Reece and the bench-clearing brawl flashed in his head, "great." He wanted to change the subject before she started asking too many questions. The rest of the family would tell her about the fight eventually. "Guess what? I'm dancing again."

"Shut up! You are not."

"I am. For a middle-school fundraiser."

"Middle school? Really? That doesn't sound like your scene."

"It's not, but … " In his mind's eye, he saw Helen Anne's smiling face, "it's better than I expected." Before Ana started wheedling details out of him, he changed the subject again. "I talked to *Mamá* the other day. She was bitching about the gig not having a big enough table for sewing. She asked me to come get her."

"She was probably serious. I think she's ready to retire."

Nah. He couldn't imagine Carlotta without the costumes and the spotlight.

"Did you talk to Dad?" Ana asked.

Giovanni fidgeted. "Yeah. Just real quick."

"How'd he sound?"

Angry. "Why? Haven't you talked to him lately?"

"I've been busy. These kids keep me cracking."

"You're avoiding him."

"It's more peaceful that way. All he wants to do is lecture me on how I should be raising these kids and pushing them to get straight As. I'm sorry he thinks he made mistakes with us, but that doesn't give him the right to harp on me."

Oh, did he know it. "One of these days, we're both going to make him proud."

Ana was quiet for a beat. "I'm sure you will."

Giovanni pulled into the parking lot and glanced up at the red, white, and blue sign high above Federal Field. "I gotta go," he said. "I just got to the stadium."

He was still thinking about what Ana had said when he entered the stadium and Coach Slater stepped out of his office to call him in.

"I debated on whether or not I should tell you this, because I don't want it messing with your head, but if I were you, I would want to know." Coach paused long enough to make Giovanni squirm. "Two scouts will be at the opening game."

Hope surged. This was what he'd been waiting for.

"They're technically coming to see the leftie who'll be taking the mound for Johnstown, but I don't see why they can't come for one guy and leave wanting another. If you catch my drift."

Giovanni nodded. "I catch it!" He reached out and shook Coach's hand. "Thanks for the heads up."

"Do with it what you will."

Oh, he would. He intended to finally prove to his father and everybody else the struggle had been worth it.

Chapter Seven

The day of the Aces' home opener, Helen Anne spent most of the morning stocking the shelves with books she'd salvaged from the pipe bursting. At noon, she left Patrice in charge with instructions to close early on account of the game, and then she headed over to the school to make signs for the fundraiser.

"Do you think we need an acronym?" Stacy asked.

Helen Anne looked at the words written in glue and covered in glitter. Dancing with the Arlington Middle School Stars. "D.A.M.S.S.?" she asked incredulously. "That's not exactly appropriate for a middle school. Besides, nobody would know what it meant. This is fine."

"But is it catchy enough? I don't know. And maybe we should make more."

Helen Anne set down her glitter and looked at her friend. "Honestly, I don't want to make more. I feel bad saying it, but I just want to get out of here."

"Since when? You're always the first one here and last one to leave."

"Burnout," Helen Anne said, but she wasn't sure that was it. She felt restless lately. Like something had changed. Whatever it was, she couldn't put her finger on it. Maybe it had something to do with Jeremy's engagement.

"I mean what if we don't have enough money left?" Stacy sounded concerned.

Helen Anne refocused. "Money for what?"

"Geez. You are burned out. I was talking about the teacher wish lists. Mrs. Reardon wants a white board. Didn't you hear a word I said?"

"I'm sorry." Helen Anne reached a hand to the back of her neck and rubbed. "I guess I'm just obsessing on everything I need to do at home in order to get to this game on time." Starting with making sure Macy finished her homework.

Helen Anne glanced at the wall clock. Five minutes until the bell rang. She could manage five more measly minutes in this seat.

"Speaking of the Aces … how's dancing with the baseball stud going?" Stacy's eyes sparkled like they always did when she thought she was in for some juicy gossip. But without a couple margaritas, she was out of luck.

"Fine." Helen Anne controlled her expression while she thought of the dance rehearsal Rachel had interrupted. She'd be a lot more comfortable talking about this if she hadn't fallen asleep every night since letting her mind take things one step further.

God, it was all so sordid.

"Are you still planning on a waltz?" Stacy colored the letter D green. When she glanced up, Helen Anne nodded.

In this case, lying was better than fielding a million questions and giving people the ammunition to spend the next few weeks laughing about the idea of uptight Helen Anne salsa dancing with the sexy ball player. It was better to keep them guessing and then surprise the hell out of them.

"That's good. A waltz should get you through it without too much drama." Stacy smiled and capped the green marker. "Speaking of drama … how's Jeremy?"

"I haven't talked to him since he called about the engagement announcement."

"How did Macy take the news?"

"Better than I expected, but she won't talk about it now. I get this feeling she thinks if she doesn't talk about it, it's not happening.

But maybe I'm wrong. All I can say is … " she lifted her hand and crossed her fingers, "there's been no drama yet."

After the bell finally rang, Helen Anne met Macy at the front entrance like they'd planned. With her Aces' cap on and her overstuffed book bag pulling her shoulders back, the kid looked tough, just a shadow of the delicate toddler Helen Anne had dressed in tutus and headbands. In her hands, which sported nibbled-on nails, was a brown paper bag.

"What's that?" Helen Anne asked.

"A home-opener present. For Gio."

As they walked to the car, Helen Anne warred with an uncomfortable feeling in her chest and pressed her daughter further. "What did you make?"

"You'll see when he opens it."

The whole way home, Helen Anne gnawed on her bottom lip, and seeing the Jeep in the driveway out back amplified her anxiety. Maybe having Giovanni here at a time when Macy could be feeling even more abandoned and overlooked by her father wasn't such a good idea. Lord knew a twenty-five-year-old professional athlete wasn't going to be much more dependable.

Macy hopped out of the car and headed straight for the carriage house steps.

"You can't go barging in on him," Helen Anne said, and as much as she didn't want to, she followed.

"Why not?"

"There are boundaries we need to respect."

Macy ignored her, and knocked loudly on the door.

"He's probably already at the stadium," she said hopefully.

Macy knocked again.

"Come on. Let's go. You can give it to him after the game."

Macy's shoulders slumped, but before Helen Anne could drag her away the door opened, and Giovanni appeared. He wore his trusty Aces' cut-off T-shirt.

"Oh. Hey," he said, looking rumpled and a little confused. Either he'd been napping or … someone else was in there.

Her heart beat erratically and unwarranted jealousy rocketed through her.

"This is for you." Macy shoved the bag toward him, and he took it, turning it over in his big hands.

"What's this?"

"Open it," Macy said, bouncing on her toes.

He reached into the bag with a yawn and pulled out a picture frame.

Helen Anne craned her neck for a better look around him. She wasn't proud, but she needed to know if he'd been alone.

"Do you know what it is?" Macy asked.

"It looks like you."

That brought Helen Anne's attention back to the gift, which was a pen-and-ink sketch of Macy at bat.

"Yeah, but what am I doing?" Macy asked.

Giovanni studied the drawing. "You're batting."

"With my bat on my shoulder. Just like you told me so I can find my sweet spot."

"Cool," he said, seemingly missing the significance of the gift, but it wasn't lost on Helen Anne, and it was driven home a moment later when Macy lunged at Giovanni and wrapped her arms around his waist, throwing him a little off balance.

Rather than return the hug, he grabbed the doorjamb on either side and looked at Helen Anne with a sort of bewildered expression on his face. It was the look of a man who appeared to be nowhere near ready to be a father. That alone put the fantasies and feelings she'd been having for him into vivid perspective.

Of course, Macy didn't see that. She released the man and gazed up at him like he'd singlehandedly created the game of baseball. "You're going to win tonight."

Finally he livened up. "You can count on it." He glanced at Helen Anne. "This just might be the biggest game of my career. Scouts are going to be there. I've been preparing all week."

She wondered what Rachel would think of that.

• • •

The Johnstown Thunderbats jumped out to an early lead, and the Aces battled for six innings against a left-handed pitcher who'd earned his reputation and arguably the total admiration of the two scouts in the stands. The longer the game dragged on, the more Giovanni saw another opportunity slipping away.

If he wanted to get noticed, he needed to make something happen. Fast.

Finally a pitching change offered some relief, and in the seventh inning, Sam Sutter hit a monstrous three-run homer to tie the game. Through it all, Giovanni was acutely aware of the scouts who happened to be sitting behind home plate, two rows above Macy and Helen Anne. So far, he hadn't done anything epic. A base on balls and two singles. He'd caught a couple routine pop-ups out in center, too, including the one he'd just tossed into the bleachers to mark the middle of the ninth inning. The time was now.

As he sat in the dugout spitting seeds, he alternated his attention between watching the bottom of the Aces' lineup bat and keeping tabs on the scouts behind home plate. Every so often, his gaze wandered to Macy and Helen Anne. They looked like they were enjoying themselves.

Roy hit into a double play, and the crowd immediately started to thin with people who either thought the Aces couldn't pull it out or weren't interested in extra innings. Their loss. Two outs. Tie game. Things were just getting interesting.

Giovanni stepped into the on-deck circle and rotated his bat. He was just a few feet from Macy and Helen Anne, separated by a wall of protective netting, but he refused to make eye contact. No distractions.

He stepped up to the plate and exhaled. *Walk-off,* he thought, because those scouts weren't going home without knowing his name. And just like that, he swung and missed.

"*Ste-er-ike!*" the umpire yelled, drawing it out for three freaking syllables.

Giovanni shook it off. He shook it all off except for the only thing that mattered. Baseball. Set again, he stared down the pitcher and kept his mind clear with the help of his senses. The sounds of the crowd morphed until they were nothing but white noise. The smell of the dirt and clay and grass and lime. The weight of the bat and the layer of sweat between his batting gloves and his palms.

An off-speed pitch sailed past him wide and outside.

"Ball one!"

The third pitch was right down the center, and it jumped off his bat, hard and fast down the left field line. Giovanni rocketed around the bases, losing his helmet when he passed second, expecting to be given the signal to slide into third. But out of the corner of his eye, he saw the left fielder bobble the ball, delaying the throw by a matter of seconds. It was enough for Giovanni to think he could make it home.

He turned on the jets, bypassing third, nothing but the echo of blood and breath in his ears. When he was a body length away, he hit the dirt hard, arms outstretched, fingers reaching, his body on a crash course with the catcher and home plate. A second before he felt the hard tag on his ass, he grazed the white corner with his left hand.

"Safe!" the umpire roared, and the crowd followed.

Some of his teammates piled on top of him. The rest circled around. Nothing compared to the rush of a walk-off win, except maybe the rush of an inside-the-park home run. Especially when scouts were watching.

He came up for air, parted the pile, and stepped into the clearing behind home plate, where he looked for the scouts and instead ended up making eye contact with an elated Helen Anne and a red-faced Macy. They were on their feet, looking every bit as excited and satisfied as he was. He walked over and fist bumped them both through the netting.

This was the first time in a long time that he'd had someone to share his triumph with besides his teammates.

When he finally shifted his gaze to where the scouts had been, the seats were empty. *Shit.*

"Caceres, this belongs to you." Coach stood behind him with the home run ball.

Giovanni caught it with one hand. He looked at the ball and back at the line of people climbing the stairs to leave the stadium. The scouts were somewhere in there. He saw Macy, too, still smiling at him, and he wanted to hop the wall beside the dugout and wade through the crowd to give her the ball.

"Hang on," Giovanni mouthed.

But before he could get to her, he caught sight of the bright yellow windbreaker of one of the scouts.

Those guys weren't leaving without talking to him.

Giovanni detoured, and minutes later, he caught up with the men in the stairwell off the rotunda. "I want to be on your radar," he said. "Because I want to be on one of your teams. I don't care which or where, and I'll do whatever it takes to get there."

They didn't say much in return. They couldn't. Neither man wanted to tip his hand. But the guy in the yellow windbreaker told Giovanni to keep making standout plays and the rest would fall into place.

It was something, but it wasn't enough. Nothing short of a concrete offer would be.

After failing to track down Macy, Giovanni stopped off for a couple celebratory beers with his teammates, and around 12:30

a.m., he finally made it back to the carriage house, where he parked in the far-right stall of the three-car garage. He climbed the stairs and punched in the same code he'd been entering for almost two weeks now. Nothing happened. No lights. No beeps. Maybe the batteries were dead. He jiggled the brass contraption and tried again. Nothing. Now what?

The only thing he could do was call Helen Anne and hope she answered. If not, he would have to drive back into town and crash with Pratt.

She answered on the second ring. "I'll be right down," she said quietly.

Upstairs, in a window overlooking the yard, a silhouette appeared. Then the room went dark. A few minutes later, another light went on, this one downstairs at the back of the big house. He saw the silhouette again a second before a spotlight lit up the backyard and Helen Anne stepped out of the house.

"Sorry about this," he called. "I tried a few times and nothing happened."

Helen Anne walked toward him, a pair of wide-leg pants and an off-the-shoulder shirt ruffling in the late-night breeze. Apparently she hadn't been sleeping, which made him wonder if she always stayed up this late, and if so, what she'd been doing.

"It could be the battery," she said. "I'm not sure the last time it was changed. I have a key though." She didn't make any real or lasting eye contact as she passed him and entered the garage.

"Thanks." He followed her up the stairs, where the heat and humidity of the closed in space clawed at his skin.

Helen Anne's perky scent intensified as he climbed faster and closed the gap between. She reached behind her head and pulled her heavy hair away from her neck, draping it over her left shoulder. A glittery hoop hung from her right ear and bounced against the crisp plain of her neck. He kept walking, kept watching, mesmerized by the sparkle and hypnotized by the curvy spot where her shoulder met her neck. It was the perfect spot for a mouth.

The sweet spot.

She stopped abruptly, but he caught himself before they collided. With his hands braced on the walls on either side of him, he looked at the inches between their bodies and breathed her in. One deep breath was all it took for him to harden, and the excessive reaction puzzled him.

Too much leftover adrenaline from the game.

She pushed the key into the lock and opened the door. Stepping inside, she stretched toward the counter and left the key. "You should keep this handy until we get the batteries changed."

"Good idea," he said, slipping between her and the door, eying up her curvy backside.

She straightened. "Well, have a good night, or day technically." She took one step toward the door, and he had the overwhelming urge to make her stay.

"Wait." He reached into the duffle bag that was hanging from his left shoulder and pulled out the game ball. "Will you give this to Macy? I wanted to give it to her after the game, but I got sidetracked by the scouts."

Her expression clouded. "Keep it. And next time don't tell her to wait if you aren't coming back."

"I *did* come back. You weren't there."

Helen Anne shook her head. "Just forget it. Really. It's probably better this way. You don't need to be giving her gifts and getting her hopes up."

"It's just a ball," he said.

"This is a little girl who doesn't get much attention from her father, and I don't want her transferring those feelings to you. I'm sure you don't want that either." She frowned. "I saw the way you reacted to her hug this afternoon."

Damn. Macy was as cool a kid as he'd ever met, but he'd never seen himself as a mentor, and he didn't want the strings that came along with a family—pseudo or otherwise.

"Understood," he said, and he tucked the ball back into his bag.

"Thank you. The more casual and uncomplicated we can keep this, the better."

"Hey, I'm all for casual and uncomplicated." Which would explain why he hadn't had a serious girlfriend since college. There was something to be said for freedom and variety. But as he stared at Helen Anne who was staring back at him, he realized there was also something to be said for familiarity and convenience. "I would offer you a drink, but all I have is water and Gatorade."

She waved him off. "That's okay. I should go. It's late. You're probably very tired."

"Not really." And now that she didn't seem so miffed at him, he wanted her to stay. Just a while longer. Long enough for him to decide whether casual and uncomplicated could work for them.

Chapter Eight

Helen Anne considered her options. She could leave, which was the smart thing to do. But Giovanni was already across the kitchen, filling two glasses with ice and water. Maybe things hadn't gone well with the scouts. Maybe Rachel had gotten wind of it. Maybe he didn't want to be alone after the disappointment. She could spare a few more minutes, couldn't she?

"What did the scouts say?" she asked as she climbed onto the end barstool and propped her elbows on the cold granite.

He set a glass in front of her and took a leisurely drink from his. His eyes never left her face. "You're good when it comes to diversion tactics."

Apparently she wasn't good enough to remain undetected.

"They didn't say a lot." He leaned on the opposite side of the counter. "But they said enough to keep me hopeful. Now …, " he let the silence linger between them, "it's my turn to divert you. Why weren't you sleeping when I called? Twelve-thirty is late for most people."

"I was reading," she said, half expecting him to laugh or make fun the way Jeremy always had.

He just nodded. "How are the pipes holding up?"

"Dry, thank you. You were a real lifesaver."

"My mom used to call me a jack of all trades and a master of none," then at Helen Anne's look, he grinned and added, "but she said it in Spanish so it didn't sound as bad."

Helen Anne couldn't imagine saying something like that to Macy. "I'm sure she was just kidding."

"She wasn't," he said dryly. "My parents love madly and criticize deeply."

"I know what that's like," she said. "My mother's the same way. It sucks." But for some reason she was laughing.

"What's your father like?"

"Detached. Only now he has reason to be. I'm sure you know about the Alzheimer's."

Giovanni nodded. "That's gotta be rough."

"It is, mostly because there's nothing anyone can do to stop it."

"The brain is crazy complicated." A faraway look came over his face, and a few seconds later he said, "I majored in psych in college."

"Seriously? I would've pegged you for phys ed."

"I graduated cum laude," he said cockily.

"Wow. I'm shocked. I thought jocks were dumb." She was legitimately surprised, but she smiled so he would know she was mostly kidding.

"Just like people who read are dorks." His lips quirked.

"Exactly."

"What did you major in?"

His question took her off guard and she delayed her answer with a few more sips of water. When she couldn't put it off anymore, she said, "I didn't go to college. I got married at nineteen. All I wanted back then was to have kids."

He shrugged nonchalantly. "Macy's better than any degree, right?

She felt a pang at how easily he praised her child, but pushed it aside.

"Yes, she is … but I would've liked the degree too. I thought about enrolling after she was born, but I expected to have more kids. Missed opportunities all the way around."

"It's not too late."

She appreciated the sentiment, but ... "I'll be forty in four years. There are increased risks after forty."

He smiled. "I was talking about college."

Oh God! "Of course you were. This is why I shouldn't be having conversations with anyone after midnight."

He chuckled. "You should definitely go back to college, and you shouldn't give up on having more kids either. Follow those dreams."

It was easy for him to say. His life was one big selfish pursuit of happiness. "I don't have time for classes and homework right now, and I'm not holding my breath on the kid thing, either. My first marriage was very unhealthy, so I'm in no hurry to repeat past mistakes. This time, I'm going to do better. I want a lot more joy and a lot less pain."

He studied her with an intensity that made her uncomfortable. "Did he hurt you?"

Her exhale was shaky. "Emotionally, but he never hit me or Macy. He's too much of a coward for that."

Giovanni's cheek pulsed, and she found the reaction oddly endearing. "That doesn't make it better."

"I know that now. And I'm okay. I am."

He leaned closer, locking onto her with his amber eyes. She leaned too, a helpless moth drawn to a brilliant flame.

"The way I see it, you're better than okay."

Her resolve weakened. She didn't want him to be gorgeous, smart, *and* understanding. She wanted him to be the immature Casanova she'd created in her mind. That man she could keep at arm's length even when they were dancing.

She sat back and regrouped. "What about you? Do you think you'll ever get married or have kids?"

"Nope."

The answer she expected—even needed to hear—but his lack of hesitation still disappointed her.

"I don't want to drag my family all over the place like my father dragged me." The same shadow that appeared the last time they'd talked about his childhood slashed across his face. "It causes too much trouble."

And there was that word again. *Trouble.* Rachel had used it to describe Giovanni. Giovanni had used it to describe his childhood. Maybe Helen Anne should use it to describe whatever it was she was doing here at nearly 1:00 a.m.

"Well then … " She hopped off the barstool. "It's a good thing you've resolved to do better."

"We both have," he said, rounding the counter to stand in front of her. "Haven't we?" A slow smile chased away the shadow. "Thanks for hanging out with me and helping me burn off the excess energy."

"Anytime," she said automatically. But her breath caught as he closed the gap between them.

"Do you mean that?"

"Sure. I'm glad I could help." She rushed a smile and sidestepped him, so she could get to the door.

"This may sound crazy, but … "

She stopped with her hand on the knob and her heart in her throat.

"I've been thinking about what you said. Casual and uncomplicated." He made the words sound like a proposition. "What do you think?"

She wasn't even sure she was interpreting his meaning the right way. "I don't know."

But was there another way to interpret it?

"Sometimes dancing together leads to other things." He stood behind her and laid a hand against her hip. "All the touching"—his warm palm slid slowly over her stomach—"and breathing"—his fingers inched higher, gliding up her breastbone—"and moving in sync." He swayed, the heat of his body pressing against her back now. His voice dropped to a husky whisper in her ear. "It just happens … naturally … and nobody tries to stop it." His thumb was gliding along her collarbone now, and with every caress, the idea seemed more and more rational. More and more inevitable.

She turned her face up to him, half expecting a disingenuous expression. He was playing with her. But honest, expectant eyes connected with hers, and she felt even more rattled.

Helen Anne took a ragged breath. "Nobody could ever know," she said. "Especially not Macy."

He paused, contemplating her solemnly, then murmured softly, "Agreed."

"But I'm not agreeing … not yet." She swallowed the self-doubt. If she was going to do this, with him, she needed to go into it with a clear head. "I need to think about it."

"How 'bout you think about this?" He spun her around, pulled her against his chest, and covered her mouth with his.

• • •

With the baseball season in full swing, close to a week went by before Helen Anne faced Giovanni again. She'd had a lot of time to think, and nothing was any clearer.

"Maybe there's too much spinning and changing directions," she said, referring to the dance routine.

Giovanni's hands were on her hips, where they'd landed when she'd careened into him on her third turn under his arm. For most of the afternoon, she'd been blaming his crazy proposition for messing up the rhythm of things.

"No worries," he said. As if he hadn't planted an idea in her head that made her do nothing but worry.

"Go again?" he asked.

"Yep."

He crossed the garage to reset the music, and she stabilized herself with a few deep breaths. He hadn't flirted or tried to kiss her once today. In fact, he'd been all business. Maybe he wasn't interested after all. Disappointment rooted her in place. It was just like her to mess up an opportunity to enjoy something casual and uncomplicated.

"Ready?" Giovanni reached out for her, that smile she loved so much brightening his face. "Remember. Feel it, don't think it." He winked, and memories of his kiss torched her skin.

Do it, she told herself, *or quit claiming you want more from life when you're settling for boring and practical.*

With a fortifying breath, she ignored his open hands and stepped into him, sliding her palms up his chest, over the swell of his muscles to his broad shoulders and the thick cords on the sides of his neck. She soaked in the feel of him. Every inch traveled bolstered her confidence until she was scraping her fingernails lightly over his skin and shimmying her body against his.

"Like this?" she asked breathily.

The music started a beat later, loud and steady, but she could've sworn she heard him groan before the downbeat. His hooded eyes turned black, and he held her hips against his, letting her feel his hardened length, moving them both in sexy, sultry circles.

He folded his body over hers until his face was against her neck and his arms were clamped low around her waist. All the while their bodies rolled to an earthy backbeat she'd never noticed despite having heard the song at least a hundred times before.

This was not their choreography, but somehow her feet kept time. Somehow her body knew the drill. Maybe that was because the man could lead. He left no room for interpretation. Neither did the solid bulge inside his pants, which was now pressing against her belly.

She wanted this. She wanted him.

She held the back of his head with her fingers laced and let the music carry her away.

When the garage grew quiet again, he looked at her but didn't let her go. His face was flushed, his eyes still dark. He stole her breath with an all-consuming kiss, and whatever remained of her sanity evaporated. The next thing she knew, her hands were at his waistband, pulling his shirttails from the back of his pants just so she could feel him soft and warm against her palms.

She teased her fingers along his spine and opened her mouth wider, angling her head, giving him full access, wanting more than his tongue in her mouth, wanting more than his hands on her body.

When they parted for air, a voice she barely recognized said, "Let's go upstairs."

Surprise mixed with the desire flooding his face. "Are you sure?"

"There's a lock on the door." Before she lost her nerve, she walked over to the shelves and grabbed her phone. "And if anyone needs me, they can call … and leave a voicemail."

Her skin was littered with leftover goose pimples and her limbs were loose with lust. It felt good to be bold for a change. She looked back at him, and he treated her to a sexy smile, but she didn't get to revel in how gorgeous he looked turned on and teased, because her phone vibrated in her hand.

The number for Arlington Middle School flashed on the screen. Someone from the office was probably calling to talk her ear off about PTA. There was always the slim chance it was the school nurse, but what were the odds of that?

Still she hesitated to send the call to voicemail.

There was a limit to her newfound boldness. She couldn't take any chances when it came to Macy.

Helen Anne hit the answer button at the exact same time Giovanni came up behind her and wrapped his arms around her waist.

"Hello?"

"Helen Anne, it's Marybeth Hunter. I'm sorry to bother you, but Macy got into a little trouble today."

"What sort of trouble?" She choked out the word.

Giovanni let go and came around where he could read her face.

"She got into a physical altercation with another student," Marybeth said.

"Macy was fighting?" Helen Anne spun around on her pumps and marched across the yard and into the house, where she grabbed her purse and keys from the counter. She could barely make out Marybeth's words over the self-loathing voice that proclaimed, *This is all your fault, mother of the year!*

Marybeth wouldn't give the name of the other child. She simply said there'd been a verbal altercation that had turned physical with Macy throwing the first punch. Helen Anne was vibrating with so much emotion she couldn't see straight by the time she exited the house.

Giovanni was waiting for her. "Is she hurt?" he asked, concern lining his forehead.

God. Helen Anne hadn't even thought to ask that, although she suspected Marybeth would've led with it. "I don't think so. She threw the first punch. Can you believe that? *Fighting.* I don't know why exactly, but I'm going to find out." She was shaking so badly she dropped her keys.

Giovanni bent first and picked them up, but he didn't give them back. "Let me drive you." He was already jogging toward her car, which was parked at an angle in front of the utility garage.

She was too out of sorts to argue. And truth be told, it had been a long time since she'd had someone strong to lean on.

Chapter Nine

Giovanni stayed in the car while Helen Anne went into the school. He sat behind the wheel with his left leg bouncing like a jackhammer. There'd been a patch of time in his life when he'd been an aggressive kid. He'd had something to prove, people to shut up. All it had ever done was drag him down and set a precedent for using force to settle his frustrations. He sure as hell hoped Macy wasn't headed down the same road now.

She charged out of the school first, running ahead of Helen Anne.

Dread washed over him, and he realized he never should've come. How did he expect to help this kid when he hadn't been able to help himself?

The minute Macy saw him, her already stormy face twisted. "Why are you here?" she asked, giving him more attitude than she ever had in the cages.

"Macy Anne." Helen Anne threw herself into the passenger seat and faced her daughter. "Don't you ever talk to an adult like that again. Do you hear me?"

Macy didn't say anything, and for a minute, Giovanni thought things were going to get better, or at least calmer, but then he heard the telltale sound of crying from the backseat, and when he looked at Helen Anne, she was crying, too.

Shit. He felt helpless. He hated feeling helpless. He definitely shouldn't have come. But he was here. What could he do to help?

He took a couple deep breaths and thought back to the way his father had handled things when Giovanni had been in serious trouble as a teen. Harsh and unyielding. No conversation, just insult added to injury. He didn't imagine that would go over well now, so he took the opposite approach. "What happened?" he asked evenly.

Nobody answered him, and he wasn't really surprised. Who was he to be getting involved in this? They weren't his family. This wasn't his kid. But still …. He had to do something, so as he pulled out of the parking lot and onto the main road, he asked, "Macy, you told me before that people were being mean to you. Was that what happened today?"

Macy cried harder, and he had his answer.

Anger pulsed in his jaw, and as much as he wanted to get to the bottom of this and offer a solution, he couldn't think of what to say next that wouldn't cause more crying.

The ride home was mostly quiet, some sniffles from the backseat, a few comments from Helen Anne about self-control and getting teachers involved instead of taking matters into your own hands. She made valid points. But Giovanni had been on the other side of things, and he knew how hard it was to stay in control.

When they pulled into the driveway, he was anxious to excuse himself and escape upstairs where he could clear his head and get ready for tonight's game, but Macy sprinted into the house the minute he killed the engine, and Helen Anne remained, looking crushed.

"I'm sorry you got dragged into this," she said.

"Nobody dragged me. I went willingly." And now that he had, he wished for a way to solve the problem. With all his experience, there had to be a way he could help. "Maybe there's something I can do."

"What? How?"

He looked beyond her over the lush green grass and billowing trees. "I got into a lot of fights when I was a kid. It led to nothing but more trouble. I'm still trying to recover from it." He slid his gaze back to Helen Anne. "Maybe Macy just needs to hear from somebody who's been there. If it's okay with you, I could talk to her when she calms down."

Helen Anne shook her head, not in a refusing sort of way, but in a way that said she was still confused. "He called her a … a *dyke*. He told everyone at lunch she likes Sophia, a girl she used to be friends with in elementary school."

"Is it true?"

"Of course not!" Helen Anne looked offended. "Why would you say something like that? She's only twelve!"

"Seems old enough to me. I don't see anything wrong with it, either, if she does."

Helen Anne shoved open the door with a rush of fury, but he caught her wrist before she could leave.

"I'm sorry," he said. "I don't mean to make things worse. I'm just being honest. That boy's a jerk no matter how you look at it, but there's nothing wrong with being gay."

"She's not gay," Helen Anne snapped, and he figured he'd better back off before he ruined everything, including his cushy living arrangements.

"Okay. Then this kid is just trying to get under her skin. I've been there. I know what it feels like. Kids used to call me a faggot for dancing. The words hurt like hell, but it gets better. She'll grow thicker skin."

"I don't want her to grow thicker skin." Helen Anne folded her hands in her lap and released a shaky sigh. "I just want to protect her, and I'll do whatever it takes to do it, which is why … I'm going to pull her out of baseball. This all started with baseball."

"Don't do that." He was surprised by the urgency in his voice. "She loves baseball. She's good at it. Don't let a few mean kids take that away from her. We can figure something else out." He strummed his fingers on the steering wheel, determined to find an alternative. "What if I have Pauly Byrne come over? I'm sure she's taken a lot of crap over the years. You could get her perspective on things, and she can talk to Macy."

"Pauly," Helen Anne said, nodding. "She does seem to have it all together, doesn't she?" She wiped the back of her hand under her nose and laughed a sad little laugh. "Unlike me. God, I really suck at this parenting thing."

"No you don't." He gripped the back of her neck gently and rubbed. "Parenting is hard for everybody."

"How would you know?"

He suddenly had a very clear picture of the torture he'd put his parents through. "Because I have parents, and they lost a lot of sleep worrying about me. They still do."

Helen Anne took a few more deep breaths, which seemed to soften her, and then she said, "If you could set something up with Pauly sooner rather than later, I'd really appreciate it."

He never wanted to get involved with this woman and her child, but considering all of this, how could he not? Baseball still came first, but nobody was going to mess with a little girl on his watch.

• • •

What if Macy was gay?

As she strangled a wooden spoon and whipped cookie dough into submission, she went over the unsettling possibility in her head. Her interest in baseball alone wasn't cause for concern, but Macy was definitely different from other kids her age. In fact, slowly but surely she'd withdrawn from her old friends. No more playdates, which wasn't unusual in middle school. But, Macy didn't go to the mall, either. She wasn't asked to have sleepovers.

And that time last summer when she'd asked to have some friends over to watch a movie in the rec room? Only one kid came, a boy. Which caused Helen Anne to painfully sit through the entire action-adventure flick simply because coed "parties" needed chaperones. What if she'd read things wrong the whole time?

She stirred harder. She did not want Macy to have an uphill battle in life. Kids weren't half as cruel as adults could be. People would tease and torment her. She'd be blacklisted and blackballed. Her world would be whittled down to the people who accepted her for who she was.

Helen Anne didn't want to think about whom that world may or may not include.

Her arm ached, but she kept on battering the batter while she ran over the potential heartache in her mind.

"Darling, you're over-mixing. You're going to make those cookies too soft." Helen Anne's mother stood on the other side of the kitchen island, watching her with a modicum of concern.

Could you *love a gay grandchild?* Jackie Reed barely left the house for fear of what people would say about her husband's Alzheimer's.

Helen Anne stopped stirring. She looked down at the too-smooth, almost liquid batter and asked, "Why don't you and Dad go to church services or social events anymore?"

Jackie sighed and tucked an errant hair behind her ear. "It's too much to ask of him. You can't expect him to sit through an hour-long service."

"He sits through nine innings of baseball."

"That's different," Jackie said, her tone clipped.

"Because he can sit in a private box where nobody will stare at him and pity him, and you won't have to worry about what he might say and when he might say it?" It sounded a lot harsher outside her head.

Jackie folded her arms. "What are you insinuating? That I'm mistreating him somehow?"

"No. No!" Where was she even headed with this? "You take excellent care of him. I'm just saying … maybe we haven't helped him stay as engaged as he could be. Maybe he would enjoy getting out more and doing different things."

Jackie turned her back to Helen Anne and straightened the items on the counter. "I like having him all to myself."

Which made sense, considering the man had spent the last thirty-plus years of his life away on business more than he'd been home. But that excuse wasn't exactly healthy or completely honest.

Helen Anne squeezed the spatula and forged ahead. "Alzheimer's isn't something you need to hide." She thought of Macy. "It shouldn't change how anybody thinks of him or us."

Jackie ripped a paper towel off the roll beside the sink and dabbed it under the faucet. "Of course not. Nobody's trying to hide your father or his disease." She scrubbed at an invisible spot on the marble counter. "The only hiding being done in this house is by the person sneaking out past midnight so she can carry on an inappropriate relationship under her parents' noses."

Helen Anne gaped. "What? No. He was locked out! Nothing inappropriate happened." *Unfortunately.* "I am not having a relationship with Giovanni Caceres." She lifted a spoonful of runny batter to her mouth.

"Don't do that," her mother scolded. "It's disgusting."

Of course it was. Helen Anne dropped the spoon in the sink with a growl. "But what if I was in a relationship with him? Or with somebody even younger? Somebody who spoke English as a second language. Would that be disgusting? Would it embarrass you?"

Jackie held her hand over her heart like she'd been mortally wounded. "Where in the world is this coming from, Helen Anne?"

For once in her life, Helen Anne didn't back down. The sense of urgency was too much to resist. "I want to know. I need to know." She took a breath. "Would you still love me if I embarrassed you?"

Jackie tucked her chin and leveled Helen Anne with a wounded look. "Of course I would still love you. The divorce wasn't your most shining moment, but I never blamed you."

Helen Anne reeled from the inconsistency. But how could she fault her mother for thinking exactly the way Helen Anne had thought for so many years.

"I need to check on your father." Without any real reassurance of her unconditional love, Jackie left the kitchen.

Helen Anne breathed through the hollowness in her chest as she put the batter in the freezer to harden, but not before she grabbed a clean spoon and filled her mouth again. It was part defiance and part necessity. Food helped her think. It also helped her not think. She wasn't sure which she needed most now.

As she sucked on a few chocolate chips, she loaded the dishwasher and periodically glanced out the window to where Macy, who was still dressed in her school clothes, was tossing a baseball off the side of the utility garage. If she listened hard enough, Helen Anne could hear the dull thud of the ball hitting the brick. *Thump ... thump ... thump ... thump.*

She still hadn't made up her mind about pulling Macy out of baseball. She couldn't help but think she had bigger worries.

Could *she* love a gay child? Of course she could, but that didn't make the prospect any less daunting, and it didn't clearly point to what she should do next.

For some reason, that prompted her to take the batter from the freezer and grab two spoons from the drawer. Then she went out into the backyard and called to Macy.

"I'm practicing," the not-so-little girl said in the same terse voice she'd been using since the scuffle at school.

"I know, but I made too much batter. I thought you might like to help me eat it."

Macy eyed her suspiciously. "You always say I shouldn't eat the batter because it has raw eggs in it and I could get sick."

"Yeah, well, that's what Grandma always told me, but I've been eating the batter without getting sick for thirty years, so … " She held out a spoon. "Whaddya say to a batter break for the batter?" Helen Anne bobbed her brows as Macy finally laughed.

"You're so weird, Mom." She took the spoon and dug in.

They ate for a few silent minutes, and then Helen Anne took a leap. "How was school?"

"A necessary evil," Macy said, sounding twice her age.

"That makes me sad to hear you say that. When I was your age, I loved school."

"Because you were like everybody else."

Helen Anne gnawed on the edges of her empty spoon. Was that the proof she was looking for? "And you're not like everybody else?"

Macy made a face. "You know I'm not. That's why you keep trying to make me do things I don't want to do."

"Like?" She waited for Macy to refill, and then she dipped her spoon into the bowl.

"Invite those girls over. Play softball. Wear dresses for church. And all the frilly stuff you buy for my bedroom. I don't really like being a homeroom helper either, but whatever."

Helen Anne licked her spoon clean while she considered what her daughter had said, and in the end, she realized whether or not Macy was gay mattered a lot less than whether or not she was happy. And clearly, the child wasn't happy … *Because I refuse to let her be.*

"Macy, I don't care if you invite those girls over ever again, and if playing baseball, and wearing pants to church, and clearing your room of everything you don't want will make you happy, then let's do it."

Macy froze. "Just like that?" she asked around the spoon still in her mouth.

"Just like that." Helen Anne wrapped an arm around her daughter's shoulder and pulled her close. "This isn't about those things anyway. Not really. This is about me recognizing you aren't happy and accepting you for you. I always will. You know?" She kissed the top of her head. "No matter what. You hear me?"

Macy was quiet for a few seconds, and Helen Anne let the peace and promise of the moment fill her up until not even another mouthful of batter sounded as satisfying.

"Mom, you're so weird," Macy repeated and wiggled free from Helen Anne's embrace.

"Yep," Helen Anne said with a smile. "Which means I'm not really like everybody else either."

At least, not anymore. The truth of the realization took her breath away.

She knew now she had too much to lose by pretending otherwise. And the weirdest thing of all was she had Giovanni to thank for it.

Chapter Ten

"Nice setup you have here." Pauly walked past Giovanni and into the apartment, wearing a big smile. Off the field, dressed in jeans and a tank top, she reminded him of Tyra Banks, but any man who thought she was just a pretty face and a pair of long legs needed to be prepared to take a fastball between his eyes. "Now I know why that idiot Pratt is calling you 'the golden boy,'" she said. "Is this what you get for having a league-leading batting average?"

"This is what you get when you're lucky as hell," Giovanni said, and then he motioned her toward the kitchen, where he had rice simmering. In reality, this was what you got when the team owner wanted to keep an eye on you.

"You're too good and too consistent to be lucky."

He pulled the lid of the pot and grinned. "Okay, then maybe I'm just that good."

"Have you heard anything from those scouts yet?" she asked, taking a seat at the island behind him.

"Not a word."

"Well, you got up the guts to corner them. That's more than I've ever done."

He removed the flour tortillas from the oven and said, "You'll get there."

She shrugged. "I used to think so, but I've seen too many guys with weaker numbers get picked up instead. I'm done worrying about that crap. I just want to play the game and be better every time I step on the mound. Can I help you with that?" She pointed to the stove.

He looked at the table, which was already set, and then back to the stove, where the rice, beans, beef, and chicken were simmering. "Nope. I think we're ready to roll as soon as they get here."

"This is really nice of you," Pauly said. "You're serious about helping out a kid."

"You say that like you're surprised I'm doing it."

"I am. You don't seem like the type. Baseball first, and fun where you can find it. Right?" She grinned. "I got your number, Caceres. At least I thought I did. What am I supposed to think about you now? We have a game tonight, and we're spending a Saturday afternoon having lunch with a little girl."

Yeah, it was definitely a change for him. "I don't want her giving up on baseball. She's talented."

"Right." But Pauly was looking at him funny.

She wasn't one to say more than she needed to say in the clubhouse or the dugout. She talked baseball and game day strategies. She didn't gossip. She didn't tease. She was there to do a job, and he admired that. But he wondered if maybe she didn't expect something was going on between him and Helen Anne.

With his back to her, he said, "You may have heard I'm dancing with her mother in a fundraiser for the middle school."

"Yep. I heard that. So you've become intimately involved with the Reed family."

Interesting choice of words. He kept stirring and let them slide. "I wouldn't say that. I just happen to be ridiculously talented and generous with my free time."

She laughed. "It all makes sense now. This place is what you get for kissing ass."

Not quite, but he couldn't help but think about the kissing he and Helen Anne had been doing. Serious kissing. The kind that had almost led them upstairs. If it hadn't been for that phone call.

And once a seed was planted in his head, he wasn't the kind of guy to give up pursuit. Hopefully this meal would get everything back on the casual and uncomplicated track.

With Pauly's help, Giovanni brought the food to the table just in time for his guests to knock.

"Hi!" he said when he opened the door.

Helen Anne and Macy matched his enthusiasm.

"Did you really cook?" Macy asked, looking at his left hand, which was still wearing an oven mitt.

"I did. I play ball. I dance. I cook. See what I mean about talent?" He threw that last bit over his shoulder to Pauly, and that was when Macy saw her.

"What?!" Macy darted past him.

"Surprise," Helen Anne said in her daughter's wake. And then she added a thank you to him with the brush of her hand across his waist. The contact lasted only seconds, but it revved him up and made him look forward to being alone with her again.

Once they sat, they didn't talk much about baseball. They ate, and compliments about his food led to conversation about families.

"What about you?" he asked Pauly. "Do you talk to your family a lot?"

"If texts count, I talk to them daily." She looked at Helen Anne. "I'm from Baltimore, so I see them a lot too. They come here, and I go there." She wagged her fork at Giovanni. "He has the sisters; I have the brothers. They like to check up on me." She leaned toward Macy. "They think they taught me everything I know about baseball." She rolled her eyes. "Let me tell you something about guys. Sometimes, it's easier to let them think what they want to think and say what they want to say."

Macy's eyes widened. "Really?"

Pauly nodded. "Why should I waste my time and energy trying to educate them? If I did that, I wouldn't have any time left in the day to work on baseball. They're wrong about a lot, and they say some pretty stupid things."

Macy giggled, but then she stopped and looked at her mother. Her gaze shifted back to Pauly and she asked, "Did kids pick on you?"

"All the time," Pauly said. "Some guys still do."

"Did you let them think what they wanted to think?"

"Yep. I let them think and say whatever they want to, and I use it all to fill up my gas tank. How do you think I hit eighty miles per hour with my fastball?"

"Wow." Macy's mouth stayed open for a few seconds, and then she said, "So I should just ignore it and fill up my tank with the stuff that makes me sad?"

"That's the best revenge," Pauly said. "Just make sure you're talking to your mom about what's really going on, because the adults can sort out the rest."

Giovanni glanced at Helen Anne, and he saw the struggle in her eyes. He knew her well enough to know she wanted to fight this battle for Macy.

After Pauly's little pep talk, Macy stuffed down two more soft tacos while she peppered Pauly with questions about baseball and they talked about travel team tryouts.

"Does everyone still pitch a few innings at your age?" Pauly asked, and when Macy nodded, she added. "Then when you're done eating, and if it's okay with your mom, I can take you outside and give you a few pointers."

"Mom?" Macy asked already standing up from her chair.

"Go," Helen Anne said with a genuine smile. "I'll help Gio clean up."

When they'd gone, the relieved look on Helen Anne's face told him things were even better than he'd expected. "Thank you," she said. "You have gone above and beyond."

"You're welcome." He pulled her out of the chair and into his arms for a hug. "She's going to be fine."

"I know she is." Helen Anne pushed out of the hug and looked up at him. "The other day in the car, when you asked if she might be gay … " She paused for a breath. "I'm embarrassed by the way I reacted. I wanted you to know that. You were right to consider it—to make me consider it. So thank you for that too."

"I'm glad I could help," he said, threading his fingers through the sides of her hair and leaning in with his lips.

The kiss wasn't long or lusty, but it was satisfying all the same, and as they broke apart to clear the table, he tried to remember any other time in his life when he'd kissed someone so surely and simply.

He couldn't think of one.

She was at the sink, rinsing dishes, chattering about the perfection of his rice and the fluff of his tortillas, while his eyes roamed the curves of her hips and the curls in her hair. He couldn't hold back much longer.

"That was mouthwatering," she said.

One word proved to be his undoing. He dropped the plates on the counter and looped his arms around her waist, pressing into her from behind. "Agreed." He nuzzled her neck, licked her lobe, and slid a hand to her breast.

"I was referring to dinner!" Her breathy laugh stoked his fire. "Does talking about food turn you on?" she asked, even as she put her mouth on his.

"You turn me on," he mumbled.

More kissing, and this time, the urgency was alarming. He hooked a hand beneath her bare thigh and pulled it to his hip.

"Gio," she whispered, her hands beneath his shirt, pawing his stomach.

He wanted to take her right here, against the counter, but he knew they didn't have the time to be that bold, so he worked his hand beneath her skirt until he bypassed her panties.

She gasped when he slipped his thumb between her slick folds.

"Tell me what you want," he said.

Her breathing was shallow from her open mouth, and her head hung back. Every flick of his thumb caused her body to tense. And when he entered her with a second finger, she groaned.

"Dime que quieres," he repeated.

She grabbed onto him, whimpering as he rubbed faster, rocking against his hand with a hunger that made him hard and breathless.

"I want everything," she said, and then she shuddered, relaxing against him with her open mouth on his neck.

Everything. He wanted that too.

• • •

Sunday afternoon, Helen Anne shut herself in her father's office and made a couple overdue phone calls. The first to the school principal, where she managed to defend Macy more efficiently than she had in the heat of the moment. The second call was to the mother of the young man who had engaged Macy in the first place. That call didn't go quite as well, but Helen Anne thought she'd gotten her point across in the end.

When she looked in the bathroom mirror shortly before midnight on Sunday night, she wasn't sure she recognized herself. No makeup, hair pulled back, a broad confident smile. Was that what an orgasm did? Released the toxins? She laughed and wished she could bottle it. She laughed harder, because screw bottling it. She wanted it on tap.

Back in her room, she looked out the window, where Giovanni's apartment was dark. Maybe he was in bed already. He was leaving for a road trip in the morning. Was it too much to hope for him to be thinking about her too?

Her answer faded on memories of the way he'd made her feel. She wanted to feel like that again. What if she went to him, snuck into the carriage house and ... She shook her head at the ridiculous idea. *Creeper.* She would never invade his space like that, but the idea stirred the lingering lust in her belly. She touched her lips and let her gaze wander over the dimly lit backyard until her breath hitched when she saw him. He was sprawled out in the moonlight on a lounge chair beside the pool. She held her breath and looked closer. It was definitely him.

What if she joined him by the pool? No sneaking required. Well, she would have to sneak out of the house, past all the alarms that were in place in case her father wandered, but she could do that. She did it the night Giovanni was locked out of the carriage house, the night that had prompted her mother to lament the inappropriate relationship. It hadn't exactly been inappropriate then. Helen Anne didn't want to think of it as inappropriate now either.

Her heart pounded. Did she really have the guts to do this? To proposition a man beside the sparkling water? To make love to him beneath the stars like they were characters in a romance novel? No strings. No messy expectations. Just a pure, sinful, temporary indulgence.

Her body ached, and her hands wandered over her nightgown, pebbling her skin. *Do it*, said the voice in her head. *Be free.*

She listened, creeping through the house to the back door, where her fingers fumbled over the keypad on the alarm and then again on the secondary locking mechanism above the door. She was lightheaded with expectation, but also because she was barely breathing, feeling like she wasn't completely in control.

Had she ever done anything this crazy?

"Never," she whispered, as she stepped out into the night, embracing the fear and exhilaration.

She hurried over the cold grass and gritty pavement in bare feet.

When he saw her, he bolted upright, a look of shock on his face. "You scared me," he said.

"I'm scaring myself." She was shaking, but in her defense, the temperature had dropped considerably since she'd been outside after dinner, tossing the ball around with Macy.

He scooted back on the lounger and patted the open space between his legs. "What's wrong?"

"Nothing." But when she reached him, she could tell by the furrow of his brow and the faraway look in his eye that something was bothering him, too. "I'm sorry," she said. "I shouldn't have come out here like this. You look like you were deep in thought." She meant to walk away, but he caught her hand.

"Stay. I was thinking." He pulled her down to sit. "About you actually. And then you were right here, and I thought I was seeing things."

She slid a trembling hand up his bare thigh and let her fingertips linger beneath the hem of his shorts. Knowing he'd been thinking about her while she'd been thinking about him made her bolder. She leaned into him and pressed her mouth to his, pulling his lips between hers, teasing him with her tongue.

"I have nothing to offer you but this." He cupped her face and looked at her earnestly.

"That's okay. This is exactly what I need. It's all I want." Excitement. Possibility.

He wrapped his arms around her waist and slid her closer, nuzzling her neck with his open mouth; lighting sparks in every corner of her body.

Despite the thrill, she kept talking, rattling off thoughts as they came. "I'm the clichéd divorcée chasing after the younger man." She laughed, low and throaty, as the tip of his tongue traced the curve of her jaw. "I know it. I see it. But I can't seem to stop myself."

He gripped her chin between his strong fingers and looked her in the eyes, "*Cálla y bésame,*" he whispered harshly.

"What does that mean?"

"This," he said, and silenced her with another kiss.

Passion flooded her and exquisite pressure built between her legs. She wanted to be naked. She wanted him naked. The heated pool glistened in the moonlight behind them, but as much as she wanted to be brave and bold—as much as she was already being brave and bold—she knew she couldn't go that far with her parents and daughter in potential view, so she grabbed his hand and coaxed him inside.

In the stairwell, he pressed her against the wall, covering her mouth with his, pulling up her nightgown so he could tease the tight buds of her nipples, and then he slid her body to the steps, where she sat and he kneeled before her.

Kisses to her mouth, her neck, her chest. He suckled her nipples through the cotton, leaving wet marks in his wake. She'd never seen anything so erotic. But then he disappeared beneath the hem of her gown and rid her of her panties.

She sucked in a breath and leaned back, momentarily worried about him getting a close-up of the extra weight she wore around her waist, but it was hard to worry when he was lavishing her inner thighs with open-mouthed kisses and expertly teasing the aching spot between her legs with his fingers. Then his mouth. And his tongue. He coaxed moans from her, and she muffled them with her hand. She writhed. She panted. She looked at the wet marks on her nightgown, her nipples hard and visible, and she reached for him. Holding him still over the epicenter.

So good.

When she closed her eyes, she saw stars, brilliant flashes of light as she came apart on those stairs with his mouth between her legs. Dangerous. Reckless. The way she should've been in her early twenties when instead she'd been learning to walk on the eggshells Jeremy had left lying around. If she'd known it could've been like this …

From this point on, no more eggshells.

"How do you say take me to bed in Spanish?" she asked.

Giovanni crawled over her, a glorious smile on her face, heat in his beautiful eyes. "*Llevame a la cama.*"

She butchered it, but they were naked in bed a minute later. This time, she worshiped him with her mouth and her hands, taking him to the brink, reveling in the power, before he was sheathed and ready to enter her.

She looked up at him, his face bathed in moonlight from the window overlooking hers, and he was the most beautiful thing she'd ever seen.

He slid inside of her with a throaty sound, and she wrapped her legs around him, drawing him closer. More sexy noises slipped from their mouths as their tongues tangled and their bottom halves rolled in sync as if they were on the dance floor.

He whispered words in Spanish against her mouth, awaking the deepest parts of her.

"I love what you do to me," she said, and he groaned.

He said something else in Spanish before he held the back of her head and deepened the kiss; thrusting into her with an insistence she eagerly met. It didn't take long until he was shuddering above her, collapsing over her in a sweaty, breathy heap.

She cradled him, dragged her fingernails up and down his spine while he squirmed.

"*Gracias,*" he said, and he kissed her softly.

Now *that* she understood, and it had her fighting a wave of raw emotion.

"*De nada,*" she said, and the minute she did, he was laughing.

A second later, he excused himself to clean up, and she rolled out of bed in search of her nightgown. Only then did she realize they'd left her panties on the steps. She felt an overwhelming urge to get them, to get back into the house and into her own bed before someone caught them and ruined everything.

She was already moving toward the bedroom door when he came out of the bathroom.

"Leaving so soon?" he asked.

"I have to. You know I do."

He nodded, looking incredibly enticing in nothing but his skin. If she could just borrow a little of his confidence … or maybe he'd been right. Maybe it *would* rub off on her. After what had just happened, maybe it already had.

"I wouldn't mind doing this again sometime." She tried her best to sound nonchalant.

He grinned. "You know where to find me."

Thank God there was a concrete path between the house and the garage. Otherwise, she'd be worried about wearing out the grass.

Chapter Eleven

At the start of the new week, Helen Anne dropped a rejuvenated Macy off at school and stopped by the principal's office to address any lingering concerns about last Friday's fight. To her surprise, PTA business only sidetracked her for an extra twenty minutes, which meant she had a couple hours to kill before she had to open the bookstore. She could go in early, or she could run home and catch Giovanni before he left for his road trip.

You know where to find me.

Less than twenty-four hours later? Wasn't that a little desperate? She ignored the killjoy in her head. There was nothing desperate about taking advantage of golden opportunities while she had them.

In town, she stuck to the speed limit, but the minute she hit the rural roads, she picked up her pace. Ten minutes later, she was hurtling down the home stretch of the driveway, when she suddenly pulled up short. Sitting at the top of the circle was an overpriced Mercedes coupe and loitering on the porch ... Jeremy.

An ominous chill snaked up her spine, and uncomfortable goose pimples covered her arms. Seeing him always brought up bad memories, and the fact that he was here unannounced only increased her wariness.

He stood, shoved his hands into the pockets of his white linen pants, and walked to the top of the steps, where he could loom over her.

She exhaled and loosened her grip on the wheel, wiggling her fingers and encouraging blood flow. This did not have to be a negative experience. She'd changed since she'd seen him three months ago for Macy's birthday. She was bolder now. Stronger.

But as she awkwardly climbed out of her car and crossed the gravel drive, forcing her shoulders back the way Giovanni had taught her when they danced, she felt like an imposter.

"What are you doing here?" she asked, managing to keep the nerves out of her voice. But the minute she stopped at the bottom step, he lifted his chin and looked down his nose at her, clearly aware of her hesitation.

"My daughter lives here," he said. "Where is everybody?"

She wrinkled her face. "Summer vacation doesn't start until mid-June. Macy is at school. My parents are probably still sleeping." Or ignoring him, thinking she'd gone straight to the bookstore and he would get tired of waiting for someone to answer the door. "I meant what are you doing in Arlington?"

Even his shrug was overconfident. "My parents threw Vikki and me an engagement party Friday night."

"And you're just now getting around to seeing your daughter? You had the entire weekend."

His eyes narrowed. "I've been busy wedding planning. Rumor has it you've been busy too."

Right then, the distinct sound of tires crunching gravel came from the far side of the house, and a second later, the shiny black Jeep with the top down and Giovanni at the wheel drove by. He beeped and waved, and she could barely lift her arm as a sick feeling whirred in the pit of her stomach. She'd missed the chance to say goodbye.

"You've got to be fucking kidding me," Jeremy said, glaring at the Jeep as it faded in the distance. "He's driving my Jeep."

Helen Anne swallowed hard and struggled to make solid eye contact. "The judge said it's my Jeep. You signed off on it. Remember? Not that it's any of your business, but Rachel asked if he could use it. He plays for the Aces and lives in the carriage house." God, she hoped she wasn't blushing.

Jeremy snorted, as if anything having to do with an unaffiliated independent baseball team was beneath him. "I can't believe your family is gullible enough to waste their money on something like that. I mean, you, I can imagine. You own that joke of a bookstore. But Rachel? Rachel used to have chops." He laughed. "Glad I got out when I did."

"Jeremy, don't." Her cheeks heated as the rest of her words caught in her throat.

His eyes were slits. "Don't what?"

And in the silence that followed, she realized she hadn't changed enough ... not yet. She was a work in progress, who wasn't sure what to say that wouldn't set him off or make things worse.

"Don't talk that way about my family." The words lacked force and only made him snicker.

He waved a hand in front of his face, dismissing her. "I don't give a shit about your family. I'm here because of Macy. She called last week all upset because you were threatening to pull her out of baseball. A decision I would fully support by the way."

"Well, that's not the case anymore."

He glared at her. "Why didn't you tell me what happened at school? I have a right to know when my daughter is having problems."

"She's not having problems. She had a problem. Singular. And it's under control."

He lowered himself down one step. "You know what else she said? She said she hates you." Helen Anne winced. "She begged me to come get her and let her live with me."

The weight of the past few years, coupled with Jeremy giving voice to Helen Anne's greatest fear threatened to strangle her voice, but she managed to push through the tightening in her throat. "She's a kid. She says a lot of things she doesn't mean when she's angry."

"Maybe," he said, dropping down another step, making Helen Anne's skin crawl with the decreased distance. "But it got me thinking. She needs me in her life. She needs at least one reasonable, rational parent around." His smile was smug and sickening. "Which is why Vikki and I are moving back to Arlington. We want to give Macy the stable, traditional family life she deserves," he paused, eyes going flinty, "since I'm already legally entitled to joint custody."

That son of a bitch. He'd never so much as exercised one-tenth of the custody he'd been granted when he'd been living in Arlington, and Helen Anne had been a fool to think his lack of interest in Macy would be permanent.

She did not want to share her daughter with this man, but she held her ground and refused to be baited. "Macy will love having you around." Her voice was surprisingly steady.

Her sureness seemed to rattle Jeremy. His eyes widened for the briefest second, but then he glanced at the heavy gold watch on his wrist. "I'm meeting with a realtor at nine, but I'll be back after school to pick up Macy and take her on a couple house tours. I want to surprise her and give her a say in her new home."

Helen Anne's heart burned. She wanted to tell him no—he couldn't sweep into town and take Macy whenever he pleased. But he had rights too.

Play the game now. Talk to your lawyer later.

"Okay," she said, and his eyes widened again.

"You seem awfully agreeable today. What gives?"

"Not a thing."

Again, his gaze drifted down the driveway where Giovanni and the Jeep had been.

She told herself to stay calm. She was imagining things. There was no reason for Jeremy to suspect anything. Jeremy, of all people, thought she would die pathetic and alone.

She stepped out of his way when he headed to his car and then hurried into the house. She didn't need to look back. Helen Anne hated the fact Macy loved him, hated even more that he suddenly wanted to be a regular part of their little girl's life. But how could she stop him? He'd been a terrible husband and a mediocre father, but that wasn't enough to get sole custody no matter how badly she wanted it. Besides, she could only imagine the damage she would do to her relationship with Macy if she tried to keep her from him.

Oh, Macy. Helen Anne sank against the closed door. Maybe if she'd opened her eyes to Macy's unhappiness sooner, the child wouldn't have felt the need to run to Jeremy. But no matter what her ex had said, Macy didn't hate her, and Helen Anne was going to keep it that way. She would figure out how to live with this new reality: Jeremy and Vikki moving to Arlington, erecting a picket fence, and including Macy in Christmas photos.

She pressed a hand to her aching chest. It was only going to get worse when Jeremy began parading Vikki around town. She could hear the gossip now: *Poor Helen Anne. Still alone. Still pathetic.*

Of course, after last night, she wasn't exactly alone. Still, she couldn't parade a twenty-five-year-old jock around town as proof of anything other than a midlife crisis.

Could she?

• • •

Three days into the four-game road trip, Giovanni looked up from his phone to see Ian Pratt standing over him, swaying with every turn the team bus made on its way to the hotel.

"Caceres, you don't pay rent anymore. You're buying the first round tonight."

"You got it, man," Giovanni said.

After another decisive win in Paducah, where Giovanni went four for four with a diving catch and a laser to the plate, he felt particularly generous. Maybe that was why he answered his phone when he saw his mother's name flash on the screen.

Between his noisy teammates and the connection, he could barely hear her. So as soon as he could, he bolted to the hotel room he was sharing with Hank. Once he was flopped on the bed, he listened to her clearly detailing the still deplorable conditions of their living environment. He looked around at the outdated floral wallpaper, scratchy bedspread, and stained carpeting in his hotel room and imagined his mother's digs weren't much better than this place. Definitely nothing like the carriage house, which he missed more than he cared to admit. Living in luxury had better not make him soft. A ballplayer needed his edge.

"Is that Gio?" Rosa asked loudly in the background.

"*Sí*. Here, Rosa. Ju tell him how bad it is in hell."

Rosa grabbed the phone, and the first thing she said was, "Ana told me you're dancing again."

"Who's dancing?" his mother shrieked. "Giovanni! Ana never told me. Ju give me that phone right now!"

"Nice work," he said amid Rosa's laughter.

"Why didn't you tell us?"

"Because it's not a big deal."

He heard shuffling, and then his mother's voice rang in his ear. "Where is this dancing? What is this dancing? Why didn't ju tell me?"

"It's not a big deal," he said again. "I'm helping out with a local school fundraiser. That's it."

"When?"

"In early June. I'm just repping the team, *Mamá*."

But in his mind, he saw Helen Anne sprawled naked on his bed, her brown hair spilling over the white pillows, her full breasts and hips begging to be played with, and he knew it had morphed into something more.

"Raul!" his mother yelled, and Giovanni's stomach churned. "Giovanni is dancing again."

He couldn't decipher his father's muffled response, but he could hear his mother coaxing the man to take the phone.

"*Mamá*, it's okay," Giovanni said, but the next thing he heard was the gruff sound of his father clearing his throat.

"Giovanni."

He closed his eyes and answered, "Hey, *Papá*."

"Ju dancing? What about baseball?"

"I can do both. The dancing isn't a big deal."

"Ju need to stay focused on baseball."

"I'm coming to see you dance!" his mother shouted.

"Tell her no, *Papá*. It's just a middle school fundraiser. You guys don't want to come all the way out here to see something like that."

His father snorted. "Maybe we do. Maybe we want to come see with our own eyes how you're staying out of trouble. How 'bout that?"

"That's cool," Giovanni said tightly. "You can come check up on me anytime you want."

He had nothing to hide.

His father's voice resounded in his head as he rejoined his team at the bar, which was attached to the hotel by a filthy Plexiglas walkway. Since he'd been late to the party, two whiskey shots were already waiting for him.

"Took you long enough!" Pratt bounced a petite blond on his knee like a frat house Santa. "I bought the first round. Hank bought the second. You can get this one." He raised his arm to summon the bartender and then pointed at the shot glasses.

Giovanni could handle a few shots without making an idiot out of himself, but he kept hearing his father's voice in his head. He picked up a shot glass, but didn't drink. He talked instead, cracked a few jokes, and eventually excused himself from the bar.

"I'll be right back," he said. After he hit the restroom, splashed some cold water on his face, and shook whatever bug was trying to ruin the night's celebratory mood.

He hadn't lied to his father. Giovanni had nothing to hide, unless you counted Helen Anne, which he didn't. Fun didn't necessarily amount to trouble. A few shots when you weren't driving amounted to fun.

But the warning wouldn't die, and his stomach wouldn't settle.

On his way out of the restroom, a man blocked his path. "I was hoping I might run into you." The man offered his hand, and Giovanni almost didn't recognize him without his yellow windbreaker. "Mark Willis. I'm the Orioles' eyes and ears in indie ball."

A proper introduction this time. He grabbed the man's hand and shook. "Mr. Willis, it's good to see you again. Were you at the game?"

"I was. Nice work. I've got my eye on you, son." He tapped a finger on the side of his nose. "We may be in the market for an outfielder with a big stick real soon, so keep your numbers up and your nose clean."

"Yes, sir!"

A lot of things ran through Giovanni's mind as he headed back to the bar. The dream was getting closer. He could almost touch it. He'd never been so grateful to have his father's voice stuck in his head. Sucking down shots in front of a scout who'd just told you to keep your nose clean? Not the brightest idea. *Thanks, Papá*, he thought. The old guy's lack of faith was annoying but apparently useful, and now more than ever, Giovanni couldn't afford a misstep.

Not when everyone was watching.

Then he saw a pretty brunette in a frilly dress with her back to the door. His body reacted as if she were Helen Anne. Muscles tight. Skin warm. The adrenaline of meeting the scout catalyzed, sending excess energy coursing through his body.

When he made it back to Arlington, he knew the perfect way to burn it off.

Chapter Twelve

By midweek, Jeremy and Vikki had decided to build their dream house in Arlington, which led them to sign a month-to-month lease on a Victorian not two blocks from the bookstore. He had also consistently exercised his right to spend more time with Macy. Helen Anne was starting to feel claustrophobic.

Meanwhile, she tried desperately to follow her lawyer's advice to sit tight for now and make peace with Macy's excitement over having her father back in town. It wasn't easy, especially tonight, when Jeremy had convinced Macy to spend the night with him at his parents' house before he returned to Pittsburgh.

With her arms full of sandwiches and drinks from Pickle's Deli, Helen Anne backed into the front door of the bookstore, thankful to have her sister in town to keep her sane. Rachel sat behind the register, where she'd been holding down the proverbial fort, looking overdressed in a pantsuit and underworked, staring mindlessly at her phone.

"No mayo, right?" Rachel asked as Helen Anne slid a turkey on whole wheat across the empty counter to her sister.

"Right. Did anyone come in while I was gone?"

"Does it look like anyone came in?"

Helen Anne shook her head. "Traffic was slow before the pipe burst, but now it's dead."

"Do people know you're open?"

"Of course they know I'm open. They knew about the pipe bursting, didn't they? If there's one thing I know, it's that word gets around Arlington."

"Yeah, but people practice selective gossip here. Bad shit travels faster and lives longer than good shit."

They nodded in agreement and then bit into their sandwiches in unison.

"You know, I was thinking while you were gone, and I want to help you," Rachel said when she stopped chewing. "Just about everything I have monetarily is tied up in the team, but we can work together and create a fresh business plan to breathe new life into this place."

Helen Anne glanced around at the massive, wooden bookshelves she'd purchased at auction from the community college several years ago. She loved that they were nicked and scraped and teeming with history. Every book on those shelves had a past life too. If it were up to her, she wouldn't change a thing, but Rachel was right.

"Help would be great," she said, picking a seed from the top slice of bread. "I have a feeling I'll have a lot more time on my hands once Jeremy moves back."

"Do you really think the fifty-fifty custody will stick? I mean he'll get bored, won't he? He's never been very interested in being a father. And soon he'll be a newlywed. Plus, who wants a preteen underfoot when you're ... " Rachel crinkled her nose and apologized before she took another bite of her sandwich. "Never mind."

Every cell in Helen Anne's body minded. "No, say it. Go ahead. What did you hear and where did you hear it?"

"Well ... " Rachel paused. "Adele heard from Franny Clinton in the ticket office that Vikki is pregnant."

"Of course she is." Helen Anne battled a surge of jealousy and bit into her sandwich again. "How much do you wanna bet he ran right to the urologist for her?" After he'd belittled Helen Anne and sworn up and down for years that the blame for their fertility issues after Macy rested on her shoulders.

Her only solace was that if Jeremy was starting a family with Vikki, maybe he would back off Macy. But the solace didn't last, because the fact she was hoping for something that would ultimately hurt her daughter disgusted her.

Helen Anne reached for her iced tea and wished she had a bottle of vodka stashed beneath the counter. Right about now a little booze while she was surrounded by her beloved books sounded like the perfect way to numb the pain. She could get lost in … "Oh my god." The straw bounced against her bottom lip. "I know how to save the bookstore." She set the cup down and grabbed onto Rachel's hands. "Books and booze."

Rachel blinked. "Go on."

"What if I had a bar in here, and occasional live music, and readings, and other social events? Anything to bring people in. Macy is always on me to take books home, and I'm forever saying I'm not a library, but what if I embraced the idea of people leisurely hanging out? Eventually the sales would come. Wouldn't they?"

"I think you're onto something."

"Of course I am!" Helen Anne clapped like a kindergartener at a school assembly.

And just like that, she cared a lot less about Jeremy and Vikki. Ideas flooded her brain. "I could call it Reed's Rum House & Reading Room." She squealed. "Wouldn't that be cool? I've never been cool, but *that* would be cool."

Rachel grinned. "What is happening to you? I swear to God you look like my sister, but my sister would never suggest bringing alcoholic beverages anywhere near her precious books."

"She just did," Helen Anne said smugly.

"I know, but why?"

She shrugged. "I guess I'm just thinking outside the box lately."

And it was freeing, almost as adrenaline charged as sneaking out of the house in order to have sex in the carriage house with …

Giovanni.

The bell over the door rang, and he appeared. Like magic.

Their eyes connected for a loaded second, but then his gaze slid to Rachel, and he frowned.

"The bookstore was on my way home from the stadium," he said nervously. "I, uh, need something new to read before the next road trip."

Rachel snorted. "You don't strike me as a reader." She glanced at Helen Anne. "Looks like somebody else has been thinking outside the box, too."

• • •

Giovanni stood frozen inside the door. Coming here had been an impulsive mistake, not the alternative from another restless night at the bar that he'd been looking for.

"So what kind of books are you into?" Rachel asked.

"Sports books," he said.

Helen Anne cleared her throat and smiled sweetly. "I'd be happy to help you find something. We have a Lou Gehrig bio you might be interested in." She winked when she turned away from her sister.

His pulse revved, but Giovanni still felt like a deer in headlights. Two minutes ago, he knew exactly what he wanted, and what he wanted was simple. A private celebration on the heels of a road win and some legitimate scouting interest. But with Rachel sitting behind the counter staring at him like he'd just set fire to the trashcans out front, nothing seemed simple anymore. He should probably consider his next move carefully.

"I don't want to interrupt," he said. "I can come back."

"Nonsense." Rachel stood. "I'm going to leave you two worms to your books." She scooted out from behind the counter and hugged her sister. "Sam should be home now, too." She raised her brows, and singsonged in a very unsettling way, "Have a good night."

Giovanni nodded as she passed, still uneasy despite the implied approval from the boss lady.

When the door closed behind Rachel, Helen Anne looked at him long and hard. "You didn't really come here to buy books. Did you?"

His ego urged him forward. "Maybe I did. And I might not know a lot about business, but it doesn't seem smart to insult a potential customer."

"I stand corrected." She looked a little nervous now, toying with a strand of hair that had escaped the knot at her neck before she said, with some degree of coyness, "I'm sure I have something you'll like. Want to help me check my stock?"

She cut between the counter and him, coming within arm's reach. And that was all it took. The scent of her skin. The sound of her breathing.

He reached out and grabbed her hand, lacing his fingers with hers. Instant heat. A million times better than a cold shot of whiskey in his hand.

"You bet I do." His voice was thick with desire.

She glanced up at him through fluttering lashes and started to smile, but then a loud group passing by the storefront caught her attention. In a blink, she pulled her hand away. "People can see us."

The sidewalk and street beyond the window were empty within seconds, the group headed off to the pub across the street, but her voice had gone cold, and she folded her arms over her chest.

Giovanni reached out, letting his hands circle her hips and squeezing gently. "Who cares? All I can see is you." He leaned in, a breath away from kissing the side of her neck, when she stepped back.

Helen Anne rolled her eyes, and worry lined her forehead. "You are the biggest flirt, but this is not the time or place."

"Why? Nobody's here. What are the odds anyone's going to come in?" He regretted the words immediately.

"Yes, well, I'm going to change that," she said stiffly. "I have a plan to bring a lot of people into the store and keep them here."

"Sounds like a hostage situation. Should I be worried?"

She eyed him up again like he was a silly kid. "You know what? I know exactly why you're here. You didn't want to go back to the carriage house and stare at somebody else's four walls. Seems kinda lonely."

The pinch in his chest said she'd hit just left of the target. Most of the locals and guys with families headed straight home after being on the road. Only the single crew was headed out to the bars again. But he'd be damned if he'd admit that sort of weakness. Life on the road was engrained in him.

"I'm never lonely," he said. "I'm surrounded by dozens of people most of the time. Even when I shower." He grinned, but she didn't take the bait.

Instead, she looked at him like she saw right through him. "There are different kinds of lonely, Gio."

He bristled at the derision in her voice. She was throwing more mixed signals than a third-base coach facing a squeeze play with two outs down in the bottom of the ninth. Clearly, something unpleasant had gotten under her skin. A better man would ask what, turn the tables, and analyze her until she was smiling again. But after the conversation with Mark Willis, the only thing Giovanni wanted to be worried about was being a better ballplayer.

"I was headed to the bar across the street with some guys, and I parked right outside your store." He shrugged off her scrutiny. "I thought it would be fun to poke my head in, crack a few leaky pipe jokes, and make you blush. But since you're obviously too busy for that, I'll leave you alone." His voice rippled with irritation.

Her brow furrowed. "I'm sorry. A lot has happened this week. Laughing just hasn't been a priority."

"Laughter should always be a priority." He resisted the urge to brush the hair from her cheek, but he could no longer resist the urge to ask why she was in such a bad mood. "What happened?"

She took a big breath before proceeding. "Jeremy is moving back to town. He and his fiancée rented a house on Second Avenue, and Macy is thrilled." Her eyes widened and then closed. Another breath, and she continued. "In fact, she's spending the night with them."

Shit. No wonder she was on pins and needles. And he'd come in here all hot and bothered, eager to get his hands under that skirt.

"I'm trying to be indifferent to it all, but it's hard," she continued. How hard was written in lines across her forehead. "I guess you could say I'm kind of an expert on those different kinds of lonely." She smiled ruefully. "That's why Rachel was here. To keep me company."

He felt a little irritation towards her sister. "No disrespect, but she abandoned her post awfully easily."

Helen Anne's smile turned teasing. "Maybe she thought you'd come to take over."

The words hung between them like the very intriguing, indecent proposal he'd originally hoped to make. But with the store still open and the sun fading, the inside lights illuminated them like a fishbowl on Main Street. If she wouldn't even hold his hand, he couldn't very well lift her onto the counter and keep her company that way.

Maybe she had the same thought, because she headed back to the counter, where a couple half-eaten turkey sandwiches, drinks, and chips waited. "Tell me about the road trip. Did you win?"

"Three outta four."

"Nice. How'd you do?" She peeled the crust off one side of her bread and took a bite.

"Good enough to get a nod from an Orioles scout."

Her eyes rounded, but it took her longer to smile than he'd expected. "That's great. Really great."

"I think so. I've been working my ass off these last two years, and it finally feels like I'm making progress. You know what I mean?"

"Actually, I do. What do you think of a bookstore that sells booze?"

It was random, but he played along. "Sounds cool. Something different." A bookstore with beer at least had a shot at pulling a guy like him in off the street.

"That's what I thought." Her voice lifted and her expression brightened. "I've been trying to figure out a way to keep this bookstore open, and it finally feels like I'm making progress, like you."

"Then we should definitely celebrate," he said.

And to his satisfaction, a sparkle lit her eye. "The store doesn't close until seven o'clock. After that, I'm all yours."

He didn't want to wait that long. He sure as hell didn't want to wait long enough for her to change her mind.

He glanced around, and then settled his gaze on her pretty face. "Where do you keep those sports books?"

"Row Ten. Toward the wall." She pointed to the back of the store, a mix of curiosity and confusion, but surely she had some idea where he was headed with this.

"Could you show me?" he asked, his tone seductive.

She dragged her bottom lip between her teeth even as she smiled. "Right this way, Mr. Caceres." Prim, proper, and hot as hell in pink heels that exaggerated the swing of her hips.

At least for tonight, he hoped she didn't see a single customer.

Chapter Thirteen

Giovanni made her scream his name in Row Ten with her back against a shelf of gardening books, and then he invited her to the carriage house—to his bed—where he made her whisper his name like a prayer. Afterward, Helen Anne watched Giovanni sleep while the moon glowed brightly in the midnight sky. He was gorgeous and capable. An amazing athlete, an incredible dancer, an outstanding cook. She lengthened her legs and pointed her toes, loving the way her body felt lush and languid. Giovanni Caceres was quite possibly the perfect man. And that was a problem. How did you ever move on from perfect?

He's not perfect. Nobody's perfect, she told herself, even as the moonlight shifted through the trees and highlighted a different, even more beautiful angle of his face.

This man had been born in a different decade and raised in a time when friends-with-benefits relationships were the norm. He'd come to that bookstore for one thing and one thing only. Until last week, Helen Anne had only ever slept with one man. This thing between them did not have legs. Casual and uncomplicated. Her words, albeit twisted. He didn't want to be serious about anything other than the Orioles scout and his chances of making it back to the big leagues. He'd never pretended anything else.

She was the one having trouble understanding things.

But why? She was older, jaded. After everything she'd been through, she shouldn't want to be serious about anything other than Macy and the bookstore. Definitely not a man. Especially not so soon after her divorce. But in the stillness of the night, staring at Giovanni's gorgeous face with memories of the way he made her feel imprinted on her body, she couldn't lie to herself. She wanted serious. She wanted stable. And in her dreams, she wanted it with him.

Those dreams needed to stop before they started giving her nightmares.

She crept out of bed, gathered her clothes, and dressed in the hall, hoping she wouldn't wake him. Then she slipped her phone from the pocket of her skirt and glanced at the screen. Five missed calls from Jeremy, four texts, and a voicemail. Macy was sick and wanted to come home.

Helen Anne bolted from the carriage house and scurried across the yard with her phone pressed to her ear.

"Where the hell have you been?" Jeremy asked, sounding pissed, and he had every reason to be.

"I'm … " She pushed through the back door, nearly botching the alarm code, "home." She stumbled into the dimly lit kitchen, heart pumping, nostrils flaring, skin damp with perspiration. "I'll come get her right now." She reached for her keys on the hook by the door.

"Don't bother," Jeremy snapped. "I'm already here."

The call ended, and Helen Anne charged through the house down the main hall, where she saw headlights illuminating the driveway and spilling into the living room through the front windows.

Her heartbeat was deafening as she disarmed the alarm, opened the door, and met them on the porch.

"I called. I texted. You didn't answer." His narrowed eyes and wrinkled nose made his disapproval loud and clear.

Macy hunched beside him clutching her stomach.

"Oh, sweetheart!" Helen Anne went to her and pulled her into a hug. The child was burning up.

"Why didn't you answer?" Jeremy demanded.

"Why didn't you give her something for the fever?"

"Don't fight in front of a sick child." Jackie Reed's voice of reason wasn't any more welcome than Jeremy's disapproval. "Bring her to me, and I'll get her settled in bed."

Helen Anne glanced at her mother and couldn't believe such a wonderful night could end so horribly. She guided Macy up the stairs, where Jackie waited and said, "I'll lock up and be right behind you with the medicine."

She didn't have any intention of discussing things further with Jeremy, but he climbed the stairs, too, and rather than step aside and let him in, where he could wreak havoc with an audience, she reached behind her and closed the door.

"You weren't home. Admit it, Helen Anne."

"Fine. Whatever. Yes, I was out, but when I called you back, I was here."

"Out where? With who?"

She bit back the impulse to correct his grammar. "That's none of your business."

"The hell it isn't," he hissed. "A mother should be home when her child needs her. Not running around town with God only knows who."

Whom, she thought again, but again she let it slide. "We were married for fourteen years. You know I'm not a runaround, and Macy always comes first with me." She reached for the door, because that was supposed to be her parting shot, but before she could get inside, Jeremy scoffed.

"I guess people change," he said. "Because when Macy needed you tonight, you were nowhere to be found."

An image of Giovanni popped into her head, and a part of her felt queasy, but another part felt bolstered. "And where were you for most of the past four years when Macy needed *you*?"

Jeremy scoffed, but a second later he looked stricken.

"Exactly. Thanks for bringing her home." Helen Anne's tone was ungracious. "I'll text you in the morning with an update."

Then she closed the door in his face.

For a few blissful seconds, she savored her escape.

"Are you coming up with the medicine?" Jackie stood at the top of the steps, wearing a fresh look of disapproval.

"I'm sorry our argument woke you."

"Oh, that wasn't what woke me, dear. You didn't reset the secondary alarm when you came in … from the carriage house … again. My bedside monitor alerted me to the breach." She exhaled as if she were wounded. "Having that man here is a mistake."

No. The mistakes had been Helen Anne's. She should've checked her phone sooner and double-checked the alarms. "I'm a grown woman, Mom."

"Acting like a teenager."

And as much as Helen Anne knew she'd screwed up tonight, she couldn't help but think of all the years when she'd been proper and manageable and unfailingly mature.

"Better late than never," she said, before slipping down the hall to the kitchen cupboard where they kept the medicine.

• • •

Giovanni had been looking forward to this home stand, and so far, it had lived up to expectation. He was flying high. Feeding off the familiarity and consistency. Fueled by the sex. It was a brilliant bonus having a steady, constructive way to blow off a little steam and burn up excess energy. Whenever he found himself thinking of Helen Anne—which was a lot lately—he told himself that.

It was no big deal.

He straddled home plate and adjusted the bat in his hands while he waited for the next pitch. He wasn't thinking about anything but baseball now.

Behind him, Coach Slater had laced his fingers through the backstop netting to watch batting practice. Time to put on a show.

Giovanni cranked out three in a row.

If the Orioles were looking for a big stick, they were going to find one.

"That's what I like to see," Slater said.

A few more pitches rocketed off Giovanni's bat. Line drives. Nothing shabby about that.

As he followed the last ball down the left field line, he saw Rachel traveling the cement walk between the box seats and the upper grandstand. Three other guys were with her: GM Benny Bryant, who was easily recognized by the glare of the sun off his bald head, and another man. Both wore suits. The third guy, whose baseball cap shaded his face, wore an Aces' uniform.

Giovanni didn't recognize the frame or the gait, but a jolt of uneasiness rattled down his spine.

The next pitch sailed by him.

"What was that? Get your head out of your ass, Caceres!" Coach Mulligan stood behind the pitching screen with another baseball in his hand. "Focus."

Who was that guy?

The question hounded Giovanni as he corrected his stance, locked his eyes on the ball, and tried to tame the restlessness.

Next pitch. Pop up.

"That was crap," Mulligan said.

Giovanni hit the bat off the inner arch of his cleats and glanced at the group coming closer again. The Aces were getting a new teammate no doubt thanks to Reece's injury. Maybe that was the source of his ambivalence. He still wasn't over the loss of his friend.

"Gentlemen!" Benny Bryant stepped up to the railing ten rows above the Aces' dugout, blocking the player in question. "Gather 'round."

Giovanni took his time moving closer, and when the player stepped out from behind Benny, the world tilted.

Tuck Mason. Giovanni never thought he'd see him again. At least not alive. But the guy looked good, filling out an Aces' uni like he'd spent the last few years in the weight room instead of drug rehab.

Apparently they were both a long way from their sordid pasts, just like they were a long way from the Mets's forty-man roster. Giovanni wasn't exactly looking forward to reconnecting and closing the gap.

After the official announcement and introductions, the team milled around Tuck, offering welcomes, but Giovanni still hung back. Rachel had made it clear his past troubles were a current concern, and now one of his former partners in crime was joining the team. The timing sucked.

"Caceres!" Tuck Mason's laser gaze cut through the crowd surrounding him, and a knowing smile split his chiseled, weathered face. "Get your scrawny ass over here and welcome a brutha."

They met halfway for a hearty hug. A lot of memories—good and bad—flooded Giovanni.

"How you been?" Giovanni needed some reassurance.

Maybe he didn't need to be worried.

"I'm in fucking farm country playing indie ball. That should tell you something about the past few years." Tuck's laugh was soaked in cynicism. "Getting clean was the toughest shit I've ever been through. Not gonna lie. I didn't think I was gonna make it, but I'm here. With you. You son of a bitch!" He jabbed playfully at Giovanni's shoulder. "I still don't know how you got out of that club before the cops came."

Giovanni laughed it off, even though stomach acid was burning his throat.

Rachel was watching them. She was too far away to hear their conversation, but it unnerved him all the same.

"You look good, man," Giovanni said sincerely, but he wanted to wrap up the conversation and get away.

"You too. We need to get caught up. Compare scars." Tuck leaned in and laughed. "The good news is we have the rest of the season to do it."

A couple back slaps and elbow nudges, and Giovanni headed to home plate amid an agitation he couldn't shake. He wasn't interested in rehashing or repeating his mistakes, but his brain was already dredging up the memories.

One hot and humid night in Atlanta. Four of them called up over the course of three weeks in September. New to late-season baseball and dance clubs with VIP rooms, drowning in top-shelf liquor and crawling with beautiful women. Everywhere. Offering whatever you wanted, wherever you wanted it. He'd been too busy taking advantage of the booty buffet to get slowed down by drugs that night, but for Tuck, it had always been the other way around.

"Caceres."

His chest tightened now at the call of a female voice.

"Walk with me." Rachel was already several feet ahead of him, climbing the steps of the visitors' dugout.

He caught up with her on the warning track just past first base.

She didn't say another word until they were well into right field. "Tuck Mason's been clean for eighteen months. Somebody needed to give him another shot. I just happened to be the somebody who needed a catcher."

Giovanni nodded, unsure of how to play this. How much did she know? "Tuck's a good guy, and he's an excellent ball player."

"I didn't realize you had a history with him until Benny brought it to my attention."

Amid a fleck of panic, rationality seeped in. Three years later, what did it matter if Giovanni's name was mentioned alongside Tuck's in an incident report? That night in Atlanta might've ruined Tuck's major-league career, but it took a couple years before Giovanni self-imploded. "We were teammates for less than a season. I'm not sure that's much of a history." And none of it should change anything Giovanni had done here.

Rachel stopped beneath the numbers—320 feet—painted on the outfield wall. "We can't lose focus. We have a championship to win. If this gets in the way … if you have any reservations whatsoever, I need to know."

"It's all good," he said carefully. Or at least it would be.

Because he didn't plan on being in Arlington long enough for Tuck Mason or their sordid history to make a difference.

• • •

With Macy still sick, Helen Anne stayed home from the Aces' game. For a woman who'd never understood the allure of grown men hitting a ball with a wooden stick, it surprised her how much she wanted to be at the stadium. Of course, her interest had little to do with the actual game—no matter how she tried to talk herself out of being interested.

She gathered up the playing cards strewn around the kitchen table and tapped them to tighten the deck. "Sweetie, I think you should go to bed."

"But I'm not tired." A yawn encircled Macy's last word.

"I see that." She chuckled.

Macy pulled a sweater-knit blanket tighter around her shoulders as she studied her iPhone screen. "It's 5-4 us. Bottom of the seventh. I need to know if they win."

"You *want* to know if they win. You *need* to sleep if you expect to feel better and have a successful travel team tryout."

Macy sighed. She battled another yawn, and then her shoulders slumped in defeat. "Fine. Will you follow the highlights on Twitter and wake me up when you know the final score?"

Helen Anne agreed.

After she tucked Macy into bed and stocked her nightstand with tissues, cough drops, and a bottle of water, she went back downstairs and settled on the leather sofa in the family room. Her iPad, phone, and a cup of chamomile tea kept her company. Two sconces on opposite sides of the French doors illuminated the near side of the room and cast eerie shadows in the hallway. She reached up and turned on the brass lamp on the drum table beside her. With her parents at the game, the big house felt empty. Lonely. And there was too much space between her and Macy. Maybe she should head back upstairs and resettle in her room.

Her phone rang before she could move. *Jeremy.*

Staring at the phone as it vibrated in her lap, Helen Anne battled a chill and refused to answer. She had texted him once today with an update on Macy's illness. There'd been no changes, so there was nothing more that needed to be said, certainly nothing that needed to be said over the phone. If he wanted to tell her something, he could text her.

And he did. Five seconds later.

Answer the phone, Helen Anne. I'm going to call again. It's important.

She bounced her head off the cushion behind her and inhaled loudly as the phone vibrated again.

"Hello."

"We need to talk about the Mexican."

The harsh statement startled her. "What?" He couldn't possibly be referring to Giovanni.

"Don't play dumb, Helen Anne. That guy who's living in the carriage house and tooling around town in my Jeep. The Mexican," he said again with a sneer.

Anger tightened her voice. "It's my Jeep, and he's American."

"He doesn't look American."

"You don't look like a bigot either."

The silence was deafening.

Helen Anne couldn't remember having ever talked to Jeremy like that. Maybe the phone between them had bolstered her confidence. Maybe she was just so tired and out of sorts she didn't care. Whatever it was something felt different, and she waited for his response on high alert.

To her surprise, he didn't defend himself or blatantly attack. "Macy seems to have a lot to say about him lately."

Helen Anne hated the idea of Macy innocently talking about Giovanni while Jeremy twisted her words. What else was he saving up to use against her? This was exactly why she hadn't wanted the child spending additional time with him.

"Giovanni is Macy's hitting coach. She respects him."

Jeremy scoffed. "She doesn't know him enough to respect him."

"As a matter of fact, she does. They've been spending a lot of time together. Giovanni is a good guy. He's been a big help with Macy."

Jeremy's growl-like exhale raised the hairs on the back of Helen Anne's neck. "Is that what you call all the shit he's been putting in her head. Being a big help?"

"I don't know what you're talking about."

"He's fueling this baseball obsession. It should've been over with by now. Do you know he told her baseball is gender neutral? *Gender neutral.*" Jeremy laughed. "She doesn't even know what the fuck that means. Not to mention it's crazy. Baseball is for boys, and softball is for girls. Especially when they get to be this age. It's a pretty simple concept, but apparently they get those things confused in Mexico."

"Stop it!" Helen Anne snapped. "You're being ridiculous."

"Am I? Well, I don't care what you think. I don't want your boy toy playing daddy with my kid and fucking her up more than she already is."

Helen Anne swallowed her shock. "You are way out of line, Jeremy. There is nothing wrong with that child. Nothing!"

"Nothing that can't be fixed with a proper role model. I mean it," he said, lowering his voice to a shade shy of threatening. "I don't care what he does with you, but I don't want that guy parenting my kid."

Her free hand shook, and her jaw ached from clenching. Screw her lawyer's advice to remain calm and not engage. "*That guy* is already a better parent than you'll ever be." She ended the call and sat seething.

How could she have been so wrong about a man? How could she have thought Jeremy would make a good father? He would undo everything she'd been trying to do to make Macy feel comfortable in her own skin. If she let him. She *would not* let him. That call had been posturing. Jeremy felt threatened. And after years of being on the opposite end, Helen Anne found some satisfaction in that. But when a guy like Jeremy felt threatened, eventually there'd be hell to pay.

All she could do now was stay one step ahead of him. If he came after her—or Macy—she would be ready.

Chapter Fourteen

The first time through the choreography, they were nearly flawless. Not a word passed between them. Their bodies did the communicating. Just the way Giovanni liked it. Smooth, sultry, in sync. On the last beat of the song, when he pulled her tightly against his body, he did what came naturally and stole a kiss.

Helen Anne's eyes were heavy-lidded and her breath labored by the time she pulled away, but as reality seeped in, the worry lines returned. He'd noticed them the minute she'd walked into the garage that morning.

Now her smile looked forced, never reaching her eyes. "Go again?" she asked.

He had worries, too, and dance seemed to offer a reprieve from them, so he nodded.

But the next two run-throughs weren't the same. She lacked concentration, and their third run-through was a complete mess of collisions and missteps. They couldn't go on like this.

Giovanni cut the music and held out his hands. "Come here."

"I know. I know." She waved him off. "I'm doing terrible. I keep screwing up."

"What's bothering you? He slid his hands up her arms and rested them on her shoulders, working his fingers into the taut muscles. "Something's wrong?"

She exhaled, and the release helped to loosen her body, but the worry lines remained. "Jeremy. He's being a jerk about Macy. He doesn't want her playing baseball. He doesn't … " The wrinkles across her forehead deepened, and her lips formed a grim line. "Never mind. I'm not going to let him get to me. I'm not going to give him any power whatsoever. Let's go again."

He couldn't shake the feeling that she'd cut herself short because "never mind" had something to do with him. Then again, maybe that was just the general paranoia he'd been feeling since Tuck Mason walked back into his life and onto his team.

This time through the routine, Giovanni was the one to botch the steps, and it prompted an unexpected but welcomed teasing from Helen Anne.

"Whoa. You never mess up. I'm so bad it's rubbing off on you." But her face brightened with recognition a second later, and she asked, "What's wrong?" She mimicked his shoulder rubs, pushing her fingers into his traps. It felt too good not to go with it.

He closed his eyes, dropped his chin to his chest, and shamelessly indulged in her manipulations. How long could he stand here and take advantage of this without saying anything? Not long. Maybe he would tell her a little bit—just so she didn't stop.

"We got a new catcher," he said, tilting his head to the left while she pressed tiny circles along his neck, liquefying his upper body and making the words spill out easier. "Tuck Mason. We played together for the Mets. It's dredging up a lot of stuff."

There was a slight stutter in her movements, and he opened his eyes to find her staring at him.

"I got into some trouble while I was New York." He had no idea why he said it.

"I know," she whispered. "Rachel mentioned something about too much partying."

He reached up and grabbed her hands as much to steady himself as to steady her. "Way too much partying. Tuck was even worse. He got busted one night when we were together." Giovanni bit his cheek and shook his head. This was where he should stop. This was always where he stopped. But the kindness in her eyes and the ache in his chest urged him to keep talking. "I left the club through the kitchen. I saw an opportunity to save myself, and I took it. Tuck ended up cuffed and arrested. I can't look him in the eyes without knowing I failed as a teammate and a friend. I should've been there. I should've faced the music."

It was the sanitized version, but it still hurt like hell to relive it from start to finish.

"Have you told him that?"

"No. If I do, I'm digging my own grave." He hadn't told her the most damning part. Tuck wouldn't have had any drugs that night if Giovanni hadn't had the connections. "Tuck could get pissed if he knows the truth, and it might cause bad blood on the team. Rachel warned me about getting into trouble again. She'll decline offers on my behalf. I know she will. I can't afford to blow another chance. I *need* to get back to the majors. I need to prove to everybody I'm not a screw up. Not anymore."

His mouth was tacky. His heartbeat was faint. He'd never said those words to anyone. Hearing them out loud, they sounded selfish. Maybe they'd sounded selfish in his head, too, but he could ignore that. He couldn't ignore Helen Anne's crumpled face and concerned gaze.

Even without the complete truth, this was where she would realize she was way too good for him.

Her careful silence amplified his anxiety.

"I think you should tell him," she finally said. "If you've changed—and I think you have—then you don't have anything to worry about. People will see what's genuinely inside of you." She smiled. "Like I do." She raised up on her toes and kissed him. Soft and sweet. Lips on lips. Breath to breath.

Giovanni opened to her. No restraint. He tangled his tongue with hers and ignored the melding of their hearts.

Even with desire flooding him, he felt unworthy. Of her. Of this. He'd been selfish from the beginning, resenting the time he'd had to spend with her and her daughter, goading her into something physical just to feed his ego, trumping her worries about Jeremy and stealing the conversation spotlight today, and still she managed to see something decent in him.

He splayed his hands across her back and pulled her closer, deepening the kiss, trying to tell her how much it meant to him. How much she meant to him. Her reason. Her stability. Her faith. He wasn't going to take her for granted anymore.

As hard as it was to go against his body's reaction to her, he pulled out of the kiss. "What can I do to help you with Jeremy?"

Her lips were red and puffy from the friction, and her eyes were watery. "Nothing." She shook her head, tousling her loose curls. "Seriously. Jeremy is my problem."

"I'm going to tell you the same thing I told Macy. You don't have to face bullying alone. Talk to someone you trust. Someone who can help." He cupped her face and brushed his thumb over her swollen lips, fighting the urge to kiss her. "I can help."

A cry-like sound caught in her throat. "Please just worry about baseball. I can handle Jeremy. His bark is worse than his bite."

But she didn't look sure, and Giovanni wasn't about to leave it at that.

Somehow, some way he would get a message across to her snarling dog of an ex. If Giovanni weren't already on Rachel's watch list, a fist to Jeremy's face would make things clear. But this time, it looked like Giovanni was going to have to use his words … and make damn sure they counted.

• • •

Giovanni loitered in the locker room before his next game. Mostly because by hanging around, he might catch word of any scouts who were in the stands, and he liked the forewarning.

So far nothing today.

He sat in a metal folding chair, oiling his glove and running through on-field scenarios in his head. It really didn't matter if a scout was here or not, though, because he was going to play like the stadium was full of them anyway. That was his job, wasn't it?

When he was done with his glove, he stood and studied the schedule taped to his inside locker wall. They were closing in on the end of May. A few road trips under their belts. Eleven wins. Three losses. It was a strong start. He could see why Rachel was thinking championship. Hell, they should all be thinking championship. But it was hard to think championship when you were thinking about getting out.

Almost end of May. Giovanni was still in Arlington. What if he was still standing here in September?

"I lost a batting glove."

He looked to his right and saw Tuck, wearing that goofy grin. It reached all the way to his eyes, where the leather-like skin wrinkled deeply. They weren't the kind of creases that came from easy laughter. Hard living was written all over Tuck's face. It shone in the pinkish whites of his eyes. And guilt clawed up Giovanni's throat.

"I'm sorry," he said, but immediately he clammed up. "I haven't seen your glove." More guilt, and this time, it pissed him off. He wasn't weak. He shouldn't be weak about this. He hadn't opened Tuck's mouth and shoved drugs down his throat. "Tuck."

He stopped on his way to his locker and faced Giovanni. "Yeah?"

"Back in Atlanta … I heard the cops were on their way, so I snuck out through the kitchen." Giovanni shook his head. "I should've gone back for you."

He laughed. "Dude. We were high and stupid. We didn't know what the fuck we were doing." But there was an edge to his voice, because he knew. They both knew. The hard drugs were in the club and on the table courtesy of Giovanni's gang ties.

"I don't talk to any of those guys anymore," he said.

False friends. He'd formed an entourage to ride the rapids, and it had pulled him under.

Tuck stared at him for a few loaded moments, and then he approached. "Good for you. I mean it." He gripped Giovanni's upper arm and squeezed. "I'm clean now, and to get that way, I had to make peace with a lot of things. That night included. It sounds like maybe you could stand a little peace too. No hard feelings, man."

The high from Tuck's forgiveness carried Giovanni through nine innings of flawless ball, and when the game was over, he couldn't wait to tell Helen Anne she'd been right.

He charged out of the locker room in record time and found Macy in the corridor waiting for him.

"My mom thinks I'm in the bathroom," she said, her expression a little sheepish.

He grinned. "You shouldn't be giving your mom the slip." But maybe that would mean Helen Anne wasn't far behind.

"I wanted to show you this." She turned around, and the back of her Aces jersey was emblazoned with "Caceres" over a bold, blue "8". "Aunt Rachel got it for me."

Air zipped from his lungs. His name, his number associated with this little girl. It made him feel things. Heavy things. Irrational things. Things he had no business thinking letting alone feeling.

"Isn't that cool?" she asked.

"Very."

"I just wanted you to see it before I go. I'm leaving tonight to stay with my dad and Vikki. Just for a few days. They moved to Arlington." She smiled, and her smile grew even bigger when she said, "Grandma's having a cookout before I leave. You should come! We're going to play Wiffle ball. You can be on my team."

How could he pass up an offer like that?

• • •

"You did what?" Helen Anne parked the car in the garage and glared at her sneaky daughter.

"I know my way around the stadium. I didn't get lost."

"That's not the point." Her overactive mother's imagination drew up all sorts of seedy scenarios involving dark tunnels in the bowels of the stadium and the strangers who would take advantage of that.

"Then what is? Don't you want Gio to play with us?"

"This has nothing to do with Gio." But truth be told, it bothered her a little bit.

Jeremy would be coming to pick up Macy at the end of the evening. Helen Anne didn't want to bend to his will as far as Giovanni was concerned, but the idea of fueling his anger in any way, shape, or form—especially when he was going to have Macy to himself for three days—made her nervous. On the other hand, Giovanni lived here. Jeremy was bound to run into him from time to time, and he needed to get used to it. Just to be safe, though, Helen Anne would steer Giovanni back to the carriage house well before Jeremy arrived. Steering him could be all kinds of fun.

She bit back a smile and apologized to Macy. "It was really nice of you to ask him. I'm sure he's looking forward to it."

The lighter moment faded a second later when Helen Anne thought about Giovanni interacting with her mother. Jackie would be as civil as proper decorum warranted but as cold as she possibly could be under the circumstances.

Unless Helen Anne could get through to her once and for all beforehand.

Inside the house, Macy ran to her room to change. Jackie was already in the kitchen, pulling packages and produce from the fridge. Danny was in the sunroom, reading the news on his iPad.

Now or never. Helen Anne squared her shoulders and entered the kitchen. "Macy invited Giovanni to the cookout."

Except for the slight jerk in posture, Jackie weathered the news gracefully. "I suppose that's being polite. But do you really think it's a good idea to involve your child in this?"

Helen Anne bellied up to the counter and grabbed a tomato and a serrated knife. "Yes, I think it's a good idea to involve my child in a family picnic. And since we're Giovanni's host family, it only makes sense in her mind for him to be invited."

"And that's it? That's all she's thinking?" Jackie dropped a plastic container of ground beef onto the opposite side of the counter and stared at Helen Anne.

"Yes. She wants to play Wiffle ball with her baseball idol."

"And what are *you* thinking, Helen Anne?"

"I'm thinking I can handle this, Mom. I've handled much worse."

They both knew she was talking about Jeremy.

"Is this serious?" her mother asked quietly. Solemnly.

Helen Anne opened her mouth to say no, but the word died on the tip of her tongue. They were having sex, and sex was serious. At least it was to her. It meant something. He meant something. But none of it meant they would end up together.

Jackie glanced out the window, and when she looked back at Helen Anne, tears shimmered in her eyes. "Don't leave me." Horror twisted her perfectly made-up face a second before her chest heaved on a silent sob. "Please. I couldn't bear it. I couldn't do this on my own."

So this hadn't been about behavior and decorum? This hadn't been about Giovanni? This had been about her father? And her mother … being lonely?

Helen Anne rushed to her and held her up in a crushing hug. "Mom, I'm not going anywhere. I would never leave you to handle all of this alone."

"But if you love him … "

Helen Anne shook her head wildly. "I'm not going anywhere," she said again. "I know how much you need me."

"Jackie!" Danny's agitated voice filtered in from the sunroom, and Jackie jumped in Helen Anne's arms. She broke free, scrambled for a dishtowel, and frantically fanned her face. A second later, she was eerily composed and on her way out of the kitchen.

Helen Anne stared out the window above the sink at the leafy green trees and clear, blue sky. Her muscles were tense, and her mind was reeling. She'd meant what she'd said. She wasn't going anywhere. But she couldn't help wondering why she hadn't just made her point by telling her mother she wasn't in love with Giovanni.

Chapter Fifteen

"These teams aren't fair!" Sam flipped the plastic bat and when he caught it, he pointed it at Macy. "You set me up. You didn't tell me about your secret weapon." He shot a grin at Giovanni, who had just emerged from the carriage house after changing out of his post-game workout gear and into a pair of cargo shorts and a polo shirt.

He wanted to put his best foot forward for a Reed family picnic

Macy giggled. "You can have my mom. She's not bad in the outfield."

"Oh thanks," Helen Anne said sarcastically.

Giovanni chuckled and ignored the urge to place a sympathetic pat on her ass as she passed.

"I don't want your charity," Sam said. "Your Aunt Rachel and I will kick your butt all by ourselves."

The screen door on the big house opened and out walked Rachel with Mr. and Mrs. Reed. Giovanni corrected his posture and plastered on a smile. *Look nice. Be respectful.* It was the least he could do for his team owner's parents, the people who were letting him live here rent-free. But in the back of his mind, he thought about Helen Anne. He didn't want to embarrass her either. Not that anybody but the two of them knew exactly what was going on between them, but still. He didn't want her having any regrets.

He glanced at her, several feet away, and she was looking at him funny, wearing a dopey smirk. He narrowed his eyes in question, and she snapped her head in the other direction as if she hadn't been looking at him in the first place. *What the hell?*

"We have a secret weapon, too," Rachel said, and then she reached behind her and grabbed her father's hand, raising their arms above their heads.

"No!" Macy yelled playfully. She ran toward her grandfather. "PopPop, that's not fair. You should be on my team."

After a little more complaining, Macy accepted the teams and gathered Giovanni and Helen Anne together near the makeshift mound. "We're not kicking PopPop's butt," she said. We're just kicking Aunt Rachel's and Sam's. Got it?"

Giovanni worked the Wiffle ball around in his right hand. "Isn't that kind of hard to do if he's on their team?"

"Nope. We'll let him hit and get on base. The other two ... " Macy popped a fist into her palm, "show no mercy."

Helen Anne laughed. "She doesn't get that from me."

"I get it from PopPop and Aunt Rachel," Macy said, and Giovanni was damn glad she hadn't said her father.

Twenty minutes later, Giovanni stepped up to home plate—a folded white towel—with Helen Anne on second and Macy on first, Sam narrowed his eyes and fake-spit on the ball.

"He's a whiffer!" Mr. Reed chanted, and everyone laughed.

Even Giovanni. It may have been the first time in his life he didn't care if he got a hit.

"Choke up!" Macy yelled. She was already a few steps off the towel they were using for second base despite the rule being no lead-offs, especially for Sam and Giovanni.

"On the bag, squirt," Rachel said, and Macy inched back only to take a lead again when Rachel turned around.

Giovanni chuckled. He liked this. He liked them. Even Rachel. They made him think about his family. Maybe things would've been fun like this if they hadn't always been moving around. Ana had kids now, and they were missing out on this sort of interaction with their grandparents. One look at the joy on Mr. Reed's face and Giovanni realized his parents were missing out too. But nothing would change as long as dancing and traveling were in their blood. Kinda like baseball and traveling were in his.

He ripped one foul, narrowly missing Helen Anne's head. She gave him the stink eye. "Watch where you're aiming that thing."

"Yeah, watch where you're aiming that thing." Sam clapped and then opened his hands. "Aim it right here."

Next pitch, Giovanni swung and missed.

"He's a whiffer!" Mr. Reed said again, and Giovanni laughed. In fact, he was still laughing when he missed the next pitch.

"Strike three! You're out!" Mrs. Reed said in a tone far too proper for baseball.

Since they were only playing one out to end the inning, Macy left the base, shaking her head. When they met up on the makeshift pitcher's mound, she said, "You're not very good at this."

"There's a learning curve," Helen Anne said, looking at him sympathetically.

He shrugged. "What can I say? Today just isn't my day." But that wasn't at all true.

In the end, they tied, zero-zero, because Mrs. Reed called the game on account of burgers and dogs. At the outdoor kitchen, which ran the length of the pool, Mr. Reed commandeered the grill, but every so often Sam snuck in to adjust the heat and flip the meat.

When Mrs. Reed came out with another plate for the grill, Helen Anne asked if she needed help in the kitchen.

"Giovanni's a great cook," Helen Anne said.

He didn't miss the way her mother frowned before she smiled. "A man who can cook is always welcome in my kitchen."

Helen Anne grabbed hold of his arm, clearly excited, so he went with it. Off to the big house. Even though he felt a little ambivalent. Playing Wiffle ball with the family was one thing. Helping Helen Anne's mother in the kitchen was another.

Once he was in the house, his uncertainty was overshadowed by his surroundings. The white and chrome kitchen looked like something out of a magazine. Wide open and fully operational with multiple ovens. Separate fridges for food and wine. Separate sinks for dishes and food prep. Basically, overkill for anyone who wasn't a professional chef, but he could learn to live with the excess.

"This is amazing." He admired the six-burner stove, where baked beans simmered, giving off a hickory scent so heavenly his mouth watered.

Mrs. Reed appeared to be studying him even though her hands were busy with the potato salad. "Did your mother teach you to cook?"

"My father, actually. My mother isn't very domestic. She can sew, but that's about it. She's excellent with a needle and thread. It's an occupational hazard."

"And her occupation is?" Mrs. Reed pointed to a wooden spoon and nodded her head toward the beans.

He caught her drift and got to stirring. "She's a dancer. Like the rest of my family."

"Interesting." But now she seemed more enthralled with the potato salad she was mixing.

Across the counter from Giovanni, Helen Anne lined up wine glasses, and then with a smile, asked if he would rather have beer. She moved effortlessly around the space, opening a bottle of red and pouring each glass without wasting a drop. It was easy to tell she'd grown up here. With wealth. Stability.

"Beer," he said, and when she pulled out a pilsner glass etched with a fancy letter R, he passed. "The bottle's fine. Why dirty a glass?"

"We have a dishwasher," Mrs. Reed said.

Her raised-nose profile reminded him of Helen Anne's haughty behavior when they'd first met. He didn't need the glass, but he needed the attitude even less. "Then I'll take a glass."

That may have earned him some points with Mrs. Reed, because for the first time since he'd moved into the carriage house, she addressed him by name. "Giovanni, how are you with slicing onions? Helen Anne didn't get very far with that earlier."

Rachel blew into the kitchen from a room on the right and grabbed the serrated knife from her mother's hand. "Hell no. He's not doing anything that puts his game at risk." She used the knife to point to a stack of napkins and plastic plates. "In fact, I don't even want him in the kitchen. You can take those out and set the table."

"Yes, ma'am," he said.

Helen Anne met him at the door with his beer still in a bottle plus two more. "Will you take these out to Sam and my dad? The non-alcoholic one goes to my dad." She rotated the labels so he could see the difference.

"Got it."

She brushed her pinkie along the outside of his hand and smiled before she walked away. Heat was exchanged, and an understanding lingered. About his task. About her mother. About the missing pilsner glass. He smiled, because whatever was happening between them was making him a frigging mind reader. Maybe he could figure out a way to hone that skill and use it at the plate. Predict pitches and raise his batting average even higher.

He pushed open the screen door with his back, balancing three beer bottles and the stack of plates, and he almost lost it all when he turned around and came face-to-face with a miserable looking middle-aged man.

He'd never met the guy before, but by his visceral reaction, he knew it had to be Jeremy.

The screen door banged behind Giovanni.

The man eyeballed Giovanni's armful, and then his narrowed gaze leveled on Giovanni's face. "I don't believe we've met."

Giovanni looked past him to the grilling area by the pool in the distance. Sam and Mr. Reed were somewhere up there. Did they know Jeremy was here? He could use some backup—or at least a better buffer than some paper plates.

"I'm Giovanni Caceres," he said. "I'd extend a hand, but I don't have one free."

"No worries." The guy's wrinkled expression said otherwise. "I'm Jeremy Gardner, Macy's father."

"Dad?" Macy bounded down the slope toward the house. "Why are you here? You're early."

The pronouncement didn't sit well with Jeremy, whose jaw clenched. "What do you mean why am I here? I'm here because I'm excited to see you."

"Oh. Well … " Macy looked at Giovanni and then past him to the house. "We haven't eaten yet," Macy said. "Can I stay and eat first?"

It didn't matter that Macy wasn't ready to leave. The guy was a natural-born bully. His rigid posture and hard-lined face said he was clearly capable of pushing the little girl out the door whenever he wanted to. And that made Giovanni's blood boil.

"I do love your grandmother's potato salad," Jeremy said, turning a tight smile on Giovanni. "Of course we can stay and eat."

His anger stewed. He needed to get out of here before he said or did something impulsive and regrettable. "Excuse me," he said, walking off in the direction of the grill.

"We can carry that up for you," Jeremy said.

And before Giovanni could turn around Macy was by his side, smiling up at him like she was doing him a favor. "I can take the plates."

"Sure thing, kiddo." Giovanni passed them over and watched her sprint across the yard with his last name written across her back. The image sparked pride and the smug satisfaction of knowing Jeremy was seeing it too.

The minute she was out of earshot, Jeremy said, "Stay the fuck away from my kid. You hear me? She belongs to me."

Anger rocketed to fury as Giovanni got in Jeremy's face. "She doesn't belong to anyone. She's not property, asshole."

Jeremy shoved him, hard enough to prompt a primal, protection instinct, and Giovanni swung with his free hand as he stumbled, barely clipping the guy's jaw.

The screen door opened behind them, and Helen Anne appeared, just as Giovanni landed on his ass amid three unbroken bottles of beer.

She was slack-jawed and speechless.

"That fucker hit me," Jeremy said, holding his face like the punch had been worse than it was. "I'm calling the cops."

Rachel was out of the house next, bearing down on Jeremy like a lioness after a lamb. "Are you physically hurt or is just your ego bruised? Because I swear to God if you pull out that phone and make a big deal out of nothing, you're going to leave here on a stretcher. I can promise you that."

While Rachel backed Jeremy away with more verbal threats, Helen Anne rushed to Giovanni. "What happened?" Worry flooded her eyes as she helped him off the ground.

He was about to say, "Your ex is a psycho," when he saw Mrs. Reed standing behind the screen, horror written in wrinkles all over her face.

This was not putting his best foot forward.

• • •

Later that evening, Helen Anne went to Giovanni, wanting his side of the story. In the commotion, all she'd gotten was Jeremy's vitriol. She still had the headache to prove it. And the heartache that went along with watching a shaken Macy leave. But Rachel had been right to insist on Macy staying with her and Sam until everyone else had calmed down—Jeremy especially.

Giovanni met Helen Anne at the carriage house door. "I was provoked," he said starkly. "My only regret is not landing a better punch. He's an asshole, Helen Anne. He didn't deserve you, and he doesn't deserve Macy."

She wrapped her arms around his neck and brushed her lips across his cheek. "I know that. I never thought for a minute you'd done anything wrong."

He turned his head and captured her mouth with his. Fierce. Hungry.

Need infiltrated her core.

They could talk later, when his hands weren't hot against her skin, when his mouth wasn't sliding down her neck.

Giovanni led her to the bedroom, speaking in Spanish while he undressed her. She didn't care that she didn't technically understand the words. She could feel their meaning. In the hardening of her nipples. In the heat between her legs. Raw. Intense. Unnerving.

When he finally made love to her slow and steady atop the covers, she clung to him, never wanting it to end.

But she knew better. More than his baseball hopes and her duty to her family, this bad blood between Giovanni and Jeremy complicated everything.

In the moonlight, still inside of her, he whispered, "I think I ruined everything."

She turned her head away from the warmth of his neck and took a deep breath. "Don't say that. It'll be okay. He didn't call the police, and Rachel knows the truth. It'll all blow over. Nothing has to change."

Giovanni pushed up on his elbows and turned her face to his. In his shining eyes, she saw the doubt, but then he brushed his nose against hers and said, "Stay with me tonight."

Her mother and father were fast asleep. Macy was with Rachel and Sam. And tomorrow, Giovanni would be off to Virginia.

Why shouldn't she?

The one reason that rose to the surface of her heart made her breathing shallow. She loved him. She did.

But she wouldn't make things worse by telling him.

Chapter Sixteen

By Thursday, the dust had settled enough for Helen Anne to agree to let Macy stay with Jeremy and Vikki for the few nights they'd originally agreed upon. Even with fairly regular text messaging, Helen Anne was going crazy without her little girl. She used any excuse she could to run over to the school in the hopes of catching a glimpse of her. Split custody sucked, especially now that Jeremy had extra leverage to enforce it. Apparently he could file a police report after the fact, and he took great pleasure in informing her of that.

All this time she'd been worried about protecting herself and Macy from Jeremy's mean streak. She just wished there was something she could do to protect Giovanni.

In his nightly texts from the road, he'd recapped the Aces' victories. The drama didn't seem to be affecting his game, which was good. And after the baseball talk, more than once, the conversation had veered into steamy territory. The drama didn't seem to be affecting his feelings for her either, which was confusing. Didn't he see how serious and complicated this had become? Maybe not. He was twenty-five and biding his time until a minor-league contract appeared. He would happily walk away from all the drama soon, which made her feel worse.

Eventually, she banished the woe in consideration of whether or not a bookstore with a bar should have a children's section. She made a mental note to discuss that with the small business administration advisor who was helping her polish her business plan.

When the bell chimed, she slipped a copy of *One Fish Two Fish Red Fish Blue Fish* into the gap beside *Oh, the Places You'll Go!* and then she left the back corner of the bookstore to greet her customer.

Only it wasn't a customer. It was Jeremy, wearing a suit and a steely gaze.

"Hey," she said uneasily, wiping her sweaty palms on her Reed's Re-readables apron. "Is everything okay with Macy?"

"How much do you know about that guy?"

She exhaled loudly. "Jeremy, please let it go."

"He has a drug conviction."

She shut her mouth and steadied her breathing. Jeremy was looking for revenge. That's what this was about. She was a half second from calling him a liar when she remembered what had happened between Giovanni and Tuck. Maybe this had something to do with that. "Whatever happened, happened a long time ago," she said carefully. "It's irrelevant now."

"So you know?" His face wrinkled with disgust. "You knew and you still let him around my daughter."

"Leave, Jeremy. I don't want to have this conversation with you, and I don't want to fight—for Macy's sake."

"That's exactly why I'm here—for Macy's sake. Did he tell you about his gang connections, too?"

Again, she shut her mouth and steadied her breathing. Apparently, she didn't have all the information Jeremy had, and she didn't want it. Not this way. Information about Giovanni should come from him and him alone.

"You should leave," she said evenly. "This is not the time or place."

"Are you kidding me?" His voice rose. "I come in here with serious concerns about the kind of people who have access to my daughter, and you can't even talk about it? I'll tell you what, that makes my decisions a hell of a lot easier."

Her spine straightened. "What decisions?"

"I'm pressing assault charges on the bastard, and I want primary custody of Macy."

The air rushed out of Helen Anne's lungs along with a chilling tone. "Absolutely not."

"Vikki and I are clearly the healthier option. There's no stability with you. She's living in her grandparents' house, where she's being subjected to your father's Alzheimer's and a revolving door of baseball players with questionable morals. He attacked me!"

"You attacked him!" Helen Anne was shaking. "No matter what you managed to dig up on him, Giovanni's a good guy."

He leveled her with a cold stare. "You really are sleeping with him, aren't you?"

"That's none of your business."

"It is if my daughter is under the same roof. Jesus Christ, Helen Anne! What has happened to you? I used to be able to trust that you were at least making rational decisions where Macy was concerned, but now? After this? He's a fucking gang-banger druggie."

"Stop it!" Her voice echoed in the empty store.

Jeremy looked surprised by the outburst, and when he shook his head, she realized she'd played right into his hands. "You'll be hearing from my lawyer."

"And you'll be hearing from mine. I'm picking Macy up on Sunday like we planned," she rasped as she followed him to the door. "She comes home with me on Sunday. You got that?"

She wanted to say more, but as he pushed out of the store two women walked in.

Helen Anne rushed a smile and a greeting. Then she hurried to the back of the store. She needed a few seconds to get herself together.

She held out her shaking hands and clasped them together, squeezing. He couldn't waltz in here and threaten her like that.

After having so little to do with Macy for the last three years? She was a good mother! Her fingernails dug into her skin. And Giovanni was a good man. Drugs? Gangs? *Oh, God.* This wasn't happening.

"Excuse me," one of the women called.

"Be right there," Helen Anne answered, her voice wobbling.

She took a few deep breaths and decided to take care of her customers first. Next, she would call her lawyer, followed by a call to Rachel so the team's attorney could be given a heads up that charges may be following. And then, she would call Giovanni.

She needed to warn him. She also needed to know the complete truth about his past.

• • •

Giovanni looked at the ripped-up, bloody skin on his right elbow and tried not to wince as the trainer poked around.

"How 'bout here?" Ben asked.

Giovanni shook his head. "I'm fine. It just stings like any other grass burn." And despite his valiant effort, he hadn't even come up with the ball.

After the wound was wrapped, and he was back in his low-budget motel room, he called his mother, who'd left a message during the game, saying they'd purchased plane tickets and would be headed to Arlington for the dance competition and a couple baseball games. As many times as he'd told them not to come, part of him was looking forward to their visit. All of him would be looking forward to it, if he didn't have this Jeremy-sized black cloud hanging over his head. Ever since that picnic, he'd been waiting for the other shoe to drop.

He was just getting into an episode of *Law & Order* when his phone rang. Seeing Helen Anne's name on the screen instead of his mother's surprised and worried him. They always texted.

When he answered, she sounded tired and far away, but it was still good to hear her voice.

"Is everything okay?" She didn't answer, and his heart sank. "Is it Macy? Your dad?"

"No. No. They're fine. It's … Jeremy. Again." She paused, and in the silence, his heart hammered. "He went to the police after all and filed a report about what happened. At least that's what he said."

Fuck. This guy just didn't quit, did he? "So I'm going to be arrested."

"Not necessarily. I talked to Rachel, and she talked to the team attorney. At this point, it's up to the DA whether they pursue charges, and under the circumstances, there's a strong possibility they won't."

"But they could."

"I guess."

He drove a fist into the mattress beside him and growled.

"Gio," she said softly. "That night when Tuck got busted, you were talking about drugs, weren't you?"

"Yeah," he said, not knowing why she was bringing this up now, but feeling like he was about to be sideswiped again.

"Were you involved with drugs, too?"

He dropped his head to the wood behind him and closed his eyes. "I never took drugs. It just wasn't my thing." It was honest, but misleading. Things were already bad. He didn't want to make them worse by dredging up ancient history.

"Were you in a gang?"

He groaned. Where was this coming from? "Yes. No. I mean … it was complicated. It was also a long time ago, and it doesn't matter now."

"It does if it threatens my daughter's life."

He sat up. "I would never, ever do anything to hurt Macy … or you. You have to believe me."

There was more silence, painful silence, and then she said, "I do, but Jeremy doesn't. He's threatening to take me back to court. He wants to be the custodial parent."

"No!" Giovanni jumped to his feet and paced the room. "That's not going to happen." She had to hear all of it. She had to understand. "Listen to me, okay? This is the honest to God's truth. I got the shit kicked out of me because I was a dancer. I needed a way to make it stop, so I went to my cousin. He was in a gang, and he talked some buddies into protecting me. I did some drug running for them in exchange. Nothing crazy. Weed. Pain pills. But I had access to the guys who had access to hard stuff, and I hooked up friends from time to time. I hooked up Tuck." He rammed a hand through his hair and clenched his teeth, but kept going. "I have no communication with any of them now. Not even my cousin. And I have no contact with drugs. It's outta my life. You gotta believe me." His breath shuddered in the silence. "Jeremy can't take Macy away from you because of that, Helen Anne. You're a great mother. Any judge will see that."

"I hope so," she said, but her voice was shaky. "Rachel said the same thing. I'm just terrified. If I lose her … "

"You won't." And he knew how he could guarantee it. "I'll move out when I get back. This is because of me. He told me to stay away from his kid, and he found a way to make sure I would. I'll squeeze in with some of the other guys. I'll sleep on the floor if I have to. Whatever it takes to get him off your back."

There was a pause. "I could put you up in a hotel. Temporarily. Just until we see how serious he is."

No, thanks. Giovanni didn't want to be some gigolo any more than he wanted to be the noose around her neck. And he had to admit that it stung a little that she hadn't said no, that it wouldn't be necessary, that it was out of the question. "I appreciate the offer, but … I think we need a clean break." He heard a tiny sob on the other end of the line, and it ripped clean through to his heart. "I don't want to mess things up for you and Macy. You're … " His throat constricted, and his eyes burned, "important to me, and I couldn't live with myself if I thought I had anything to do with splitting you up."

"Gio … " She was clearly crying. "Maybe it won't come to that."

He pressed the heel of his palm to his eye. "Are you willing to take that chance?"

He knew she wasn't. A mother like Helen Anne was willing to sacrifice anything for her child.

"What about the fundraiser?" she asked. "We've worked so hard and Macy is looking forward to it."

His family was, too. So it would be a clean break except for that. "I'll be there."

"Thank you," she said.

He couldn't think of anything else to say, so he ended the call and stared at the ceiling.

The other shoe had dropped like a lead anvil.

What if he ended up suspended—or worse—because the DA decided to pursue charges? What if his family came all the way to Arlington only to learn he was exactly what they'd feared he was? What if he somehow ended up costing Helen Anne Macy?

No. He couldn't let that happen. He wouldn't let that happen.

As soon as he got back to Arlington, he would go to Rachel and lay it all on the line. He would ask for a trade instead. It wouldn't save him from a possible arrest, and it wouldn't be easy starting over. Hell, it could wreak havoc on the rest of his season. But it was the only way he could think to get Jeremy off Helen Anne's back for good.

Chapter Seventeen

Helen Anne put the finishing touches on Macy's end-of-year gifts for teachers. The twinkling Mason jars were supposed to be a mother-daughter joint effort, but ever since Giovanni had returned to town but not the carriage house, Macy had been blaming Helen Anne for everything.

"You should tell her what's going on," Rachel said, looking up from her tablet-sized phone. "She's old enough to understand."

"No." Helen Anne over-tightened the ribbon she was fluffing and shook her head. "I don't want her to think less of him."

"Jeremy or Giovanni?"

"Giovanni." Definitely Giovanni. The more Helen Anne thought about things, the less she cared about the trouble he'd been in years ago. He'd proven himself over the last few months to be a good man and a responsible man. Jeremy on the other hand …

"You're a better woman than I am. I'd tell her exactly what kind of asshole her father is, and I would let Jeremy wallow in his own mess."

If there was a way to accomplish that without backlash, you bet she would. That's why she'd been wracking her brain trying to come up with some leverage of her own. But so far, nothing came to mind. And she was clearly running out of time.

"I can't believe Giovanni asked for a trade." She placed a finished mason jar in a partitioned cardboard box.

"I can. He loves you."

Helen Anne choked out a laughed. "Please."

"I'm serious. He knows a trade wouldn't stop the cops from coming after him if the DA decides Jeremy's charges warrant it, so he wasn't asking to save himself. He was asking to save you. To save Macy. Even though a trade at this point in the season would raise some eyebrows and potentially negatively impact his play. Think about that for a minute. He was willing to risk his career to protect you."

Helen Anne stared at Rachel in disbelief. Could it be true? "No," she said. "I'm sure he feels responsible, but that doesn't mean he … " She couldn't even say the words.

"What if he does?"

"He *doesn't*."

"Would it change anything?"

Everything. Hope built and then crashed. *Nothing.* Because even if they could make a long-distance relationship work, Jeremy would make their lives a living hell.

She glanced up and out the window at the empty carriage house and flushed with anger. She needed to find a way to end this cycle once and for all.

"What's wrong?"

"I keep letting Jeremy win without putting up a fight. It's like I know I'm going to fail, so I accept the loss up front. That's why I let him have the house on Pine Avenue. Because I was afraid of losing the bookstore."

Rachel shrugged. "I don't see it like that. The bookstore was more important to you."

"No! It wasn't *more* important." She could feel her blood thickening. "I loved that house. I decorated that house. I rocked Macy to sleep in that house. I planted every flower around that house. Both places were equally important to me, but I didn't fight for them equally." She growled. "Why didn't I fight for them both? Why did I think I had to give in to get anything at all?"

Rachel gave her that distant look that was part detachment and part apology, both parts the result of Rachel not being there when things had fallen apart for Helen Anne. "I don't know what to say. It's too late now. Jeremy sold the house on Pine Avenue years ago. You signed off on the divorce terms. I guess you could … "

"This is not about the house!" Helen Anne slapped her hand on the table, and Rachel jumped. "I'm sorry. I'm so sorry."

"Don't you dare apologize," Rachel said. "Own your feelings. You're entitled to every last one of them. If it's not about the house, then what's it about?"

Helen Anne took a big breath. "Giovanni and Macy are both important to me, but I didn't fight for them equally." That sounded crazy, didn't it? Macy was her daughter, and she was supposed to come before everyone else. "I know people will say that makes me a bad mother. I know people will say my child should always, always come first. But … " She struggled to find the right words. "For once, I want to put myself first, and to do that, I need both of them, because I love them both."

Rachel nodded, seemingly taking it all in, and Helen Anne didn't flinch. She didn't worry about Rachel passing judgment, mostly because Rachel wasn't that kind of woman, but also because—surprisingly, refreshingly—in this moment, Helen Anne no longer cared.

"He's leaving," Rachel said, solemnly.

Helen Anne's stomach bottomed out. "What? I thought you said you refused his request for a trade."

"I did. In part because an Orioles affiliate contacted Benny. Nothing's settled, and it's strictly confidential at this point. Giovanni doesn't even know."

"Oh." Helen Anne's anger mixed with confusion. Why had Rachel let her get carried away?

"I wasn't going to tell you until it was settled, either, but after what you just said … you need to find out if he feels the same way about you, and you need to do it soon."

"So I can stop him from leaving? Isn't that what you've been hoping to get out of this all along? You want him to stay to win you a championship."

Rachel's expression was matter-of-fact. "I made no secret about that in the beginning. It's true. But right now, after everything, I'd give up a championship to see you live happily ever after. Seriously. Talk to him for you, not me."

"But maybe I'm crazy. Maybe I should be more worried about his past."

"Helen Anne, if you of all people aren't really worried about his past, then that's because there's nothing to worry about. People change. They grow up. We did." She smiled.

"True. But that just means all my worries are focused on the future. Like whether or not he's even going to be here much longer."

"Why does it have to be about him staying in Arlington? As much as I'd love to keep him here. Why couldn't it be about you leaving with him? Don't you ever think about living outside of Arlington?"

Helen Anne let that rattle around in her head for a split second, but then her mother's tortured expression took its place. "I promised Mom I wouldn't leave her. Besides, I would have to get court approval to take Macy out of state. Can you imagine the fight over that? Plus, the bookstore is here, and I'm really excited about rebranding it."

"Okay, so you live in Arlington and visit Giovanni whenever you can. When the school schedule allows, you take Macy with you. While you're gone, I'll do the heavy lifting with Mom and Dad. And in the off-season, Giovanni can come back to Arlington and spend it with you. Baseball is filled with crazy relationships like that. You just have to commit to making it work."

Actually, there was something she needed to do first.

She had to tell the man she loved him.

• • •

Flatbush Brewery was hopping thanks to the bluegrass pickings of a bearded duo, who had one hell of a following. Smack dab in the middle of cowboy boots and flannel shirts was a table full of Venezuelan-American dancers, who'd never quite learned the meaning of "toning it down."

"Ju' need suntin' here and here." Giovanni's made-up and bejeweled mother tapped one blood-red fingernail beneath his eyes. "Too dark. Are you sleeping?"

"Yes, *Mamá*. I'm sleeping." But not soundly. That was impossible to do on an air mattress in equipment manager Quincy Marshall's three-season room, which was four feet from the tree where an industrial-size bug zapper worked itself into a frenzy every night. And every night, when he was shocked awake by the sound of another meaty moth frying, he stayed awake, cursing Rachel for not approving a trade and staring at the ceiling, wondering how long it might be before he was arrested and how long it might take to stop missing Helen Anne.

"Ju' need concealer." She snapped her fingers. "Rosa."

Rosa plopped her shiny pink purse on the table and began rummaging through it.

"I don't need concealer," he snapped, but then he smoothed it over with a smile. "Baseball players don't care about that crap." And for now, he was still a baseball player.

"Fans care what you look like," his father said, patting Giovanni soundly on the thigh. The simple movement caused a cloud of spicy cologne to rise up in the space between them. "What if one of these pretty women wants to take a selfie with you?"

Lucia snickered.

Helen Anne was the only pretty woman he cared to think about.

He glanced at his phone, which contained a text she'd sent earlier that day. She wanted to see him. To talk to him. Despite the clean break, he wanted that, too. But he still worried about Jeremy. He wanted to keep things calm while his family was here. If all hell was going to break loose, he hoped it would wait until they were on the plane.

"I can't wait to see you play ball," his father said.

"And dance," his mother said, patting his thigh.

He answered with a smile and then glanced at his phone again.

"Nobody dances here?" his mother asked, and before he could answer, she was on her feet. "Raul, *vamonos*."

His father hopped up, and soon they were dancing in a patch of open space near the restrooms. *Papá* in his shiny black pants and *Mamá* in her ankle-length flamenco skirt.

"Oh, God," Lucia said. "I don't mind the foxtrot, but if they start to cha-cha, I'm outta here."

Rosa and Giovanni laughed, but Giovanni's laughter caught in his throat when he saw a familiar face in the distance just beyond his father. Helen Anne worked her way through the crowd alongside Rachel and Sam. Dressed in a boldly printed dress that tied around her neck and dropped to her feet, she looked confident and radiant, and he couldn't drag his eyes away.

"What?" Rosa spun around.

"What'd they do?" Lucia asked. "Did he dip her?"

With a flip of her long hair, Helen Anne settled into a booth across the room without ever noticing him. "It's fine," he said. "It wasn't them."

When he finally pulled his gaze away from Helen Anne and looked at his sisters, Rosa was looking back and forth between him and the booth across the room.

"Is she somebody you know?" she asked with one sculpted brow raised.

"Who?" Lucia was looking now too.

"I don't know," Rosa said. "Either the blonde or the brunette."

"The brunette," he said. "She's my, uh, dance partner."

"Is she?" Rosa grinned. "Well, I'd like to meet your, uh, dance partner."

"Can we?" Lucia asked.

Giovanni looked at his parents who had somehow inspired a few other less-coordinated couples to join them on the makeshift dance floor. His family had a way of making everything a big deal. Was he ready for this? Did he have a choice? His sisters were as bold and pushy as his mother. If he didn't introduce them to Helen Anne, they wouldn't hesitate to waltz over and introduce themselves.

"Fine," he said. "But play it cool. She's with her sister, who owns my baseball team. And her sister's boyfriend is our first baseman, Sam Sutter. Trust me. I've brought enough drama into their lives recently, and I don't need you guys stirring up any more trouble."

Lucia nodded sincerely.

Rosa batted her lashes and crossed her heart. "I'll be the perfect angel."

He doubted that, but still, he led her toward them.

When Sam saw Giovanni approaching the table, he stood with an outstretched hand. "Hey, man."

Helen Anne glanced over her bare shoulder and her eyes widened.

Just the sight of her had his heart pumping harder.

"I wanted you all to meet my sisters, Rosa and Lucia."

There were formal introductions followed by some small talk about dancing, baseball, and even Macy. Every once in a while Giovanni stole a glance at Helen Anne and wished they could have five minutes alone.

"Do we get to meet your parents, too?" Rachel asked, and Giovanni hesitated.

"Sure!" Rosa said.

Maybe Lucia picked up on Giovanni's hesitation, because she swept into the conversation with an excuse. "They're in the zone right now. It could be a while before they sit back down."

Speaking of sitting back down … Giovanni tried to think of a way to wrap things up. Fortunately, a waitress toting a tray of food made for the perfect excuse. As they said their goodbyes, he couldn't help himself—he let his hand rest on the seatback of the wooden booth where his thumb grazed Helen Anne's neck. It was quick and covert, but as they left the table, Rosa eyed him up, bobbing her brows. She'd seen; she knew.

Giovanni ignored her.

Halfway to the table, his father reached out and pulled Lucia into the dancing circle.

That left Giovanni and Rosa to return to their table. The minute they sat, she said, "So 'my, uh, dance partner' means 'the woman I'm sleeping with.'"

Thank God his parents were still on the dance floor. He barely noted they'd moved on to other partners before he attempted to shut down the conversation. "It was nothing major."

"Nothing major?" Rosa looked Helen Anne's way again. "How old is she?"

"Older," he said, his tone clipped.

"I'm not saying she looks old, Gio. She's very pretty. Naturally pretty. Classy. She just doesn't look like the kind of woman who would do 'nothing major.'"

He stole a glance at Helen Anne, who was sipping from her wine glass. His heart pinched. "Yeah. I know."

"So what's the problem? Are you bothered by her age?"

"No."

"Her kid?"

"Hell no."

"Then what's the problem?" She said each word slowly and clearly. "'Cause it's clear you still want to be with her."

"I lost my cool around her ex-husband, and now he thinks I'm a bad influence."

Rosa laughed. "Imagine what he would think if he saw you in full makeup and a leotard. Talk about a bad influence."

He wished he could laugh. Instead, he leaned closer and lowered his voice. "I punched him, Rosa, and he filed a police report. He also dug up the drug conviction."

"I thought juvie records were sealed."

"Me, too."

"Did she wig out when she heard that? She looks like she would wig."

"No," he said, remembering the phone call. "She was sad, but calm. I was the one who wigged out. I ended things." Rosa stared at him, and he added, "I care about her. And her kid. A lot. I didn't want to cause them any trouble."

"Do you love her?"

He made a face. "Let's talk about something else."

Rosa kicked him under the table. "Talk to a lawyer, Gio. I don't know why you punched him or what filing a police report entails, but maybe the juvie record won't matter. I mean, it shouldn't matter. Not now. And it definitely shouldn't keep you away from the woman you love."

"You're crazy," he said, affectionately, and then he looked to the dance floor where the rest of his family was cha-cha dancing while the band sang some song about getting drunk on a plane. The Caceres were all crazy. Him included, because when he glanced at Helen Anne again, he decided talking to an attorney wasn't such a bad idea.

Chapter Eighteen

Giovanni arrived at the stadium for Friday night's game two hours ahead of time. He bypassed the stairs to the clubhouse and took the elevator to the administrative floor, where Administrative Vice President Ray Fenton's office sat three doors down from Rachel Reed's door.

Giovanni walked tall. He had nothing to fear. Fenton was an attorney who regularly helped guys navigate personal and professional dilemmas.

He knocked on the ajar door.

"*Entre Vous*," Fenton bellowed, complete with an exaggerated French accent.

Giovanni had never dealt with the guy before, but he'd heard he was quite the character. Now, he was seeing that firsthand.

"Good to see you, son." Fenton stood up and extended a hand. He looked to be in his sixties, which made sense, because Giovanni had heard the man was a longtime friend of Mr. Reed's. He wore white slacks, a plaid sport coat, and a bowtie. All that was missing was a hat and cane.

"Thanks for seeing me," Giovanni said. He took a seat when one was offered. "Any time," Fenton said. "That's what I get paid for. Now, what can I help you with?"

Giovanni squared his shoulders and dove in. "I was sort of hoping you had some experience with family law."

Fenton leaned back, and his leather chair creaked and groaned. "Did you get somebody pregnant?"

"No, sir. Nothing like that."

"Fall behind on child support?"

"No, sir. I don't have any kids."

"That you know of." The man laughed. "A little pro-athlete humor."

Which wasn't in the least bit funny. "No. I'm one-hundred-percent certain I'm no one's father. This is about … someone else's kid. I was involved with a single mother until her ex-husband … " He paused. Fenton wasn't the official team legal counsel, but something told Giovanni he already knew about the punch, which meant he might also know about Helen Anne. "Let me start again. When I was fifteen, I was charged with possession, sale, and intent to distribute marijuana. I ended up with probation and community service, and later I had the record sealed. Somehow her ex got hold of that info. And now he's threatening her with a custody battle if she continues to see me. I'm just wondering if he has a case."

Fenton nodded. "This is the guy you socked? The one who filed a police report?"

Giovanni nodded.

"Well, you're batting a thousand with this one, aren't you, son?" He laughed again. "Honestly, complicated custody questions are beyond my scope, but I can make a few calls and find you the answer."

"I would appreciate that."

"You're sure she's worth the aggravation?"

"Yeah," he said wistfully. She had to be, because nothing had felt right since he'd insisted on a clean break. And seeing her yesterday only made him want to see her again.

Fenton left a couple messages for attorneys he knew around town, and finally, the third call resulted in another lawyer on the phone.

Giovanni held his breath while Fenton laid the groundwork for the guy. At this point, he wasn't sure how he wanted things to go.

If this guy came back with information that gave him the green light to pursue Helen Anne, would that change anything?

"Mind if I put you on speakerphone?" Fenton asked.

Apparently, the guy agreed, because soon Giovanni was listening to a faceless man say, "Worst case scenario your juvenile record will be admissible, and then it will be weighed against the kind of man you've been since. Having an arrest warrant issued for assaulting this child's father will make everything worse. But if that doesn't come to pass, things look a hell of a lot brighter. In cases like this, your adult life acts as your resume. Your college record will be scrutinized. Your employment record. Your personal and professional accomplishments will come into play. It all tells the court the story of who you are today. You'll most likely be allowed character witnesses, too. Coaches. Colleagues. Professors. Pastors. Whoever can paint you as the kind of man people would be proud to have around their children."

So there was a chance he could be with Helen Anne and not put her relationship with Macy at risk. As long as he kept his nose clean. It always came back to that, didn't it? Funny, under the circumstances, he was more motivated to do that than he'd ever been.

Giovanni sat there unable to move, feeling heavier than he had five minutes ago. He never should've thrown that punch. But he couldn't take it back, and he wasn't sure how to move forward. Jeremy wasn't exactly the kind of guy you could reason with. Besides, actions spoke louder than words. Positive actions. Being the kind of man people would be proud to have around their children was more important than being a baseball player.

He'd never given it much thought before. Baseball had been his life, his identity, the way he intended to prove he was someone his family could be proud of. But what if he'd been wrong? What if clawing his way back into the Majors wasn't enough anymore?

• • •

Saturday morning, Helen Anne jolted awake from a dream in which she'd just fallen off the Arlington Middle School stage and had become the laughing stock of the town.

Someone was standing at the foot of her bed.

"Macy?" She squinted as she fished for her glasses on the nightstand. When she pushed them on and could see clearly, she saw her daughter dressed in the clothes she'd worn to bed, a tattered Arlington Softball Association T-shirt and cotton shorts that were two sizes too small. Macy was clutching the stuffed bunny Helen Anne had given her for her sixth birthday. And in that moment, none of the distance or aggravation of the last week mattered.

"What's wrong, baby?" Helen Anne asked, pulling back the covers and motioning for Macy to crawl into bed. "Did you have a bad dream?"

Macy shook her head, but she climbed over Helen Anne's legs and into bed all the same. As she burrowed under the covers and nestled into Helen Anne's arms, she said, "I was just thinking."

"Thinking about what?"

"Something I heard."

Helen Anne sighed as she kissed her daughter's head. "What did you hear?"

"It's not what you're thinking."

"What am I thinking?"

"You're probably thinking I'm getting picked on again."

Helen Anne nodded. "I hope that's not it."

"It's not. Somebody was kinda picking on Gio, though." Macy looked up then, and the uncertainty in her eyes made Helen Anne's stomach clench.

"Who? What did they say?"

"Dad," she whispered, and Helen Anne felt her face burn. "I heard him talking to Vikki, and he called Gio … " Macy swallowed as if what came next was hard to digest, "a scumbag."

Helen Anne exhaled. Scumbag wasn't as bad as some of the things she'd been imagining. And "scumbag" wasn't as scarring as "druggie." Of course, neither one was true, and she wasn't going to let Jeremy ruin Giovanni's reputation, especially where Macy was concerned. "Sweetie, your father doesn't even know Giovanni. He's just, well, jealous about all the time we were spending with Gio."

"But he has Vikki. He spends all his time with her. Why would he be jealous we found someone new?"

We. One word that meant absolutely everything. They really had picked Giovanni as a pair, hadn't they? Helen Anne pulled her daughter closer and kissed her head again. "Your father is a complicated man, Macy. He didn't like being with me, but apparently he doesn't like me being with anyone else."

Macy seemed to think about that while Helen Anne wished for better words to explain this frustrating situation.

"Like the time you gave my old bike to Ally Timmons, and when I saw her riding it, I wanted it back even though I really didn't?"

"Exactly," Helen Anne said with a small smile. "But your dad doesn't want me back. He just wants to make sure he's not going to lose you."

Macy's face wrinkled. "He's not going to lose me. I'm his kid."

Helen Anne laughed. "You're one smart cookie, you know that?"

"I know that," Macy said with a grin.

"It's just going to take some time for your dad to know that."

"Well, I wish he would hurry up, because I want Gio to come back."

"Oh, sweetie. So do I, but I don't think that's going to happen." Especially not after what Rachel had told her. Without giving too much away, she had to make Macy see that. "One of these days, he's going to sign with a big-league team, and you can't expect him to walk away from that."

Macy dropped her head to Helen Anne's shoulder and was quiet for a few long seconds before she said, "We could go with him."

Helen Anne closed her eyes and imagined a world where they could be so free and easy, but then she opened her eyes and faced reality. "What about PopPop? What about school? What about the bookstore? What about your dad?"

Macy sighed. "Good points. Dad would really be sad then, wouldn't he?"

Sad and angry. And as much as Helen Anne hated having to play nice with a man who couldn't seem to play nice with her, she wouldn't take Macy away from her father.

"So we just let Gio leave?" Macy asked.

"There's an old saying: If you love something, set it free. If it comes back, it's yours. If … " She stopped short, feeling foolish for waxing poetic around Macy. "Never mind. I can't remember the exact words. The point is we can't make him stay here without making him sad, too."

"I guess," Macy said, still sounding unconvinced. "Maybe you should tell him anyway."

"Tell him what?"

"That you love him. That … " she turned her face into Helen Anne's shoulder and offered a muffled, "we love him. It would nice for him to know."

For a split second she thought about denying the obvious, but she couldn't think of a way to do that without making light of Macy's own courageous admission. For some reason, that clarified and solidified a few things. Helen Anne had been stalling.

No more.

"I'll tell him," she said. "I'll find a way."

• • •

When Helen Anne saw Giovanni striding toward her through the throng of people gathered backstage at Arlington Middle School, her first thought wasn't, "I love him," it was, "Please don't let me fall off the stage." That dream had done a number on her.

But then he smiled, and the buzz in her blood burned off the nerves. He was breathtaking, dressed in sleek, black trousers and a fitted white shirt that smoothed across his broad chest and deepened the tone of his skin.

"Hey," he said. His tone was pure velvet, and when he took her hand, she melted, leaning against him for a hug that was the only thing keeping her off the ground.

She breathed him in and out, losing herself in the intoxicating mix of spicy cologne and magnificent man. She loved him in the scariest way imaginable. The way that made you want to put it all on the line, when you knew you had way too much to risk.

"Gio," she whispered, and his arms tightened around her waist a second before Stacy called out her name.

Helen Anne lingered.

"Look at you two!" Stacy said.

Helen Anne stepped away from Giovanni and tried not to look guilty, but her skin was clammy, and her heart was beating triple time, and Stacy was looking at her like she was a middle schooler with a high-school-sized crush. She was guilty as hell, and she was tired of hiding it. Yes, she loved this man. Jeremy had been right; she had no shame. But he'd also been wrong, because there was nothing pathetic about it.

Helen Anne stepped closer to Giovanni and smiled brightly at Stacy. "Is there a good crowd out there?"

"Amazing! I think we're going to have the biggest budget on record to start next year." Stacy crossed her fingers. "White boards for everyone." She giggled. "But first, you guys need numbers."

She handed Helen Anne two sheets of paper and safety pins. "Fasten them to your backs so the judges can see them. And good luck." She winked.

When she was gone, Giovanni said, "I have a good feeling about this." He was looking at the numbers in Helen Anne's hands. That's when she saw it, too.

"Number 8. That's your number. That's crazy. It's a total coincidence."

"I don't believe in coincidences," he said, slipping an arm around her waist and pulling her closer despite the movement all around them. "Not anymore. Everything happens for a reason."

She looked up at him, a lump in her throat and the words in her head. *Tell him. Tell him now.* At this point, what did she have to lose?

"Break a leg," a familiar voice called, and Helen Anne blinked. That was all it took to pull her out of the moment.

Lester and Amity walked by, all smiles despite the fact that he looked incredibly awkward dressed in black from head to toe with his hair slicked back. Amity fared better in a white, fit-and-flare dress, but her Dirty-Dancing-inspired bob was obviously a wig. If it weren't for the assistant principal and his partner, who were standing near the exit dressed as Tarzan and Jane, Helen Anne would've thought Lester and Amity had taken things a bit too far. Instead, she looked down at her own red dress and matching heels. Maybe they'd downplayed the importance of giving a flashy performance.

"Don't worry about it," Giovanni said, squeezing her gently. "Our dancing will speak for itself."

And just like that, the butterflies in her stomach refocused on the dance.

For the next twenty minutes, they stood off in the wings with the rest of the participants. Giovanni enjoyed the show through a split in the curtains, while Helen Anne tried to remember every step, every move, every count in her head, which was impossible with other peoples' music blaring from the sound system.

By the time their number and names were called, she was a nervous wreck.

"We got this," he said as he took her hand and marched her into the spotlight amid a ridiculous roar from the crowd.

Her stomach churned. Her knees buckled. Her vision blurred. She thought she'd seen Macy out there, but now she couldn't tell.

He spun her around, adjusted their hands and with a blazing smile said, "Look at me. Only me. Feel your way through it."

She had no other choice, because as the noisy gym quieted, the music began.

For the first few eight counts, she did everything he'd told her to, except she miscounted once and nearly misstepped, but she caught herself at the same time she caught the twinkle in his eyes and the hitch of his lips. He held her tighter, guiding them both in daring lines and salacious circles around the stage. Finally, miraculously, she relaxed. She stopped fighting. She stopped trying to get everything right. And in that moment, she was free. The wind from their quick movements ruffled her hair, and a happy thrumming beat in her heart.

When the last notes of music faded, she remained suspended in Giovanni's strong arms, his body bent over hers, his face inches away. When he smiled amid audience cheers, she lost herself to the moment, raising her hands to either side of his face. In one breathless, joyous motion, she pulled her lips to his and couldn't have cared less who was watching.

Chapter Nineteen

Helen Anne hadn't found a way to tell Giovanni she loved him, but that kiss probably made things a little clearer … to him, the entire school, half the Aces' baseball team, and both sets of parents. Her face burned. She should've picked a subtler way. But on the heels of that salsa dance, subtle was a joke.

While Tarzan and Jane claimed their first-place trophy, Helen Anne and Giovanni made their way through the crowded gym to their families. Helen Anne's initial instinct was to avoid making eye contact with anyone, but with Giovanni's hand resting hot and strong on her lower back, she felt bolstered. And when heads turned in their direction, she dug deep, stood taller, and met their inquisitive glances with a smile. It was time to turn pity into envy—friendly envy. She'd waited a long time for this.

Reaching behind her, she grabbed Giovanni's hand and held it proudly for all to see.

Eventually, he veered off toward his family after brushing a kiss across her knuckles. Helen Anne headed for her own with a flutter in her chest.

"Mom!" Macy leaped toward her. "You were amazing!"

"Thanks, honey."

"I especially liked the ending," Rachel said with a wink. "Everybody did."

Well, maybe not everybody. Helen Anne looked at her mother. "Too showy?" she asked.

"Some things are better left in private," she said stiffly, but a second later her face softened. "Aside from that, you did a wonderful job, dear. He's certainly a talented young man."

"Who?" Helen Anne's father asked, and when he was reminded of the dance competition and Helen Anne's participation, his face brightened. "You look beautiful. Did you win?"

"No, Dad. We got second place."

His face wrinkled, because no matter what the Alzheimer's did to his memory, he was still a man who valued winning.

"You should've won," Rachel said. "Or maybe you should've worn some stupid costume, because that judging was suspect. Next year it shouldn't be so subjective."

"Next year," Sam said to her, "we're going to get you up there. I would pay millions to see you salsa."

Rachel laughed. "Thank God we don't have millions."

They shared a look that said they had something better than a big fat bank account, and Helen Anne found her gaze wandering over the crowd to Giovanni. She made eye contact with his mother, instead, and the room closed in on her. What had Mrs. Caceres thought of the dance? The kiss?

Helen Anne wasn't sure she wanted to know, but then the dazzling woman raised her fingertips to her lips in salute.

A warm blush of gratitude swept across Helen Anne's cheeks, but she turned cold with nausea a second later when she realized Giovanni and his family were headed her way.

Macy saw him, too. She broke through the crowd and ran to him, grabbing his hands and spinning under his arms while he laughed. He seemed to be introducing her to his mother, father, and sisters. Helen Anne took a few deep breaths. She wanted them to love Macy more than she wanted them to love her.

"Cute," Rachel said from somewhere behind her.

Once the Reeds and the Caceres were introduced, conversation turned to dancing, and Helen Anne relaxed until her father's short-term memory issues became too jarring to ignore.

"It was lovely meeting all of you," Jackie said, taking Danny by the arm and prompting him to say goodbye, too.

After a brief explanation of her father's diagnosis, the conversation turned to dance again, with Giovanni telling stories about their early rehearsals. While he joked about her initial stiffness and reservations, he complimented her profusely. Maybe more than he should have, because his father, who'd been mostly a quiet observer, said, "I fell in love with my wife while we were dancing."

Helen Anne was sure her face registered the shock of being called out by that statement, but Giovanni just smiled. As the air crackled between them, she felt like she was standing on the precipice of something big, something huge, something ...

He broke eye contact suddenly and pulled his vibrating cell phone from his pocket. For a few seconds, he stood frozen, an unreadable look on his face. "I, uh, I have to take this." And then he left the gym, leaving a sense of unrest in the middle of what had been a joyful gathering.

"Maybe it's the minor-league scout he was telling us about," Lucia said.

Helen Anne and Rachel exchanged glances, but Rachel kept quiet.

"Ju must be right!" Mrs. Caceres raised fisted hands to her lips in excitement. She spoke her next few words in Spanish, opening her hands and raising them toward the ceiling. If Helen Anne wasn't mistaken, something about Jesus had been mentioned in there.

Mr. Caceres wrapped an arm around his wife's shoulders, closed his eyes, and kissed her temple. "*Gracias a Dios.*"

"He told you he would do it, *Papá*," Rosa said. "He's going to make you proud again."

Helen Anne found herself silently praying too, because she couldn't bear it if the caller was the team attorney giving Giovanni a heads-up about an arrest warrant.

At this moment, all she knew for sure was whoever was on the other end of that call had the power to change everything.

• • •

For five minutes, Giovanni wandered up and down the school hallway while Mark Willis explained his interest. There was a roster spot in the Orioles farm system. Single A. Willis said it was a foot in the door. After that, it would be up to Giovanni to sink or swim.

He'd been waiting for this call. He'd been dreaming about this chance. But it felt anticlimactic somehow. Because of a middle school dance? No. But ten minutes ago, he couldn't stop smiling, and now he'd broken out into a cold sweat.

The offer to buy out Giovanni's contract would be made within a couple weeks. At that point, it would be up to the Aces' front office to accept or decline. Rachel had already refused a trade. Maybe she would refuse a buyout too.

There was a surprising indifference in his heart when he thought about that. In fact, all he cared about right now was that he wasn't quite ready to leave Arlington. Things were ramping up on the field. A championship was in reach. And then there was Helen Anne.

He thanked Mark Willis for calling, then he sat on the steps overlooking the playground. If the Aces agreed and he accepted the buyout, he would be back at the bottom again, scraping his way to the top in unfamiliar towns amid unfamiliar faces. Desperate to prove himself. With no guarantees. He could be cut again. The endless circle seemed daunting.

What if he stayed? He didn't have to give up baseball in Arlington. Not yet at least. He couldn't play indie baseball for the rest of his life, though, and he could never support a family on those wages. Not that he had a family to support. But lately he'd been thinking about it. Seriously. What if? Staying in Arlington would give him a real shot at having *everything*.

By the time he returned to the gym, the Reeds had left for Macy's rec game, and in a way he was relieved. Helen Anne would've seen right through him, and he wasn't really ready to explain himself to her.

"So?" His mother was bouncing on the balls of her stilettos. "Do we celebrate?"

The expectation on their faces almost changed his mind, but he couldn't make this decision just to please them.

He took a big breath and nodded. "We celebrate." As his sisters and mother rushed to hug him, he added, "But for a different reason."

His father's gaze sharpened. "What does that mean?"

"I guess it means I think I'm going to try something different now. I want to stay put in Arlington and grow some roots. I'm ready for more than a baseball career."

His mother squealed and squeezed his face between her hands. "I knew it! Ju love her!"

He did. This decision made that clear.

"So no baseball?" his father asked solemnly. "What will you do?"

"I'll keep playing here in Arlington, *Papá*, for as long as I can, and I'll work around town in the off-season."

His father frowned. "What kind of life is that? Ju have a college degree. Use it."

Giovanni did have one of those, and he knew how important it had been to his father who didn't even have a high school diploma. Giovanni on the other hand had never put much stock in his education. It had been something he'd done on the side while he was playing baseball. But thinking about it now gave him an idea. To pursue a career in psychology he'd need a master's degree, so why not go back to school?

"You're absolutely right." He broke through his mother and sisters to reach his father for a bear hug. "I'm going to use my degree, *Papá*. I'm going to use it to go back to school and get another one."

"*Mi hijo loco*," his father said between laughter. "*Estoy orgulloso de ti.*"

Giovanni didn't half mind being called crazy when the very next thing his father said was that he was proud.

Chapter Twenty

Helen Anne hated that she couldn't wait around in the gym to find out who had called Giovanni and what it was all about, but she understood why hanging around could get awkward, and she'd thanked Rachel for encouraging her to leave. On the way to Macy's late-afternoon rec game, Helen Anne and Rachel kept things quiet, but the minute Macy jumped out of the car with her bat bag in tow, the floodgates opened.

"Shit," Rachel said. "Benny just texted. The Orioles single-A affiliate will have an offer for Giovanni's contract by the end of next week."

The call hadn't been about the punch and a warrant. *Thank God.* But a second later, Helen Anne's relief succumbed to reality.

"So are you going to let him go?" she asked, her voice strained.

"You know I don't want to, but I'm not really the bitch people make me out to be. When it comes down to it, I can't imagine trouncing his dream, unless … " She bit her lip and eyed her sister. "I would decline the offer for you. Just say the word"

"No," Helen Anne said quickly and easily. "God no. He wants this. He deserves this."

Rachel reached over, grabbed her hand, and they sat there in silence, staring at the field.

"Just because he's leaving doesn't mean I'm going to stop loving him," Helen Anne said. "I meant what I said. I'm going to fight for him. I'm going to find a way to make this work."

"Definitely," Rachel said, brighter. "And just because he's leaving doesn't mean I'm going to stop working toward a championship. There are thirty-eight other guys on that roster."

A few more silent but powerful seconds ticked by, and then Jeremy and Vikki walked past hand in hand.

"It doesn't seem fair. Does it?" Rachel asked.

"Not at all," Helen Anne said.

And she finally felt compelled enough to do something about it.

She was out of the car before Rachel could stop her, but she heard the passenger door slam a beat after hers.

"Jeremy!"

He turned, and the minute he saw her, his features hardened. Vikki maintained her composure and kept a hold on his hand.

"Helen Anne," he said, sounding wary.

She ignored him, giving a genuine smile to Vikki. None of this was her fault, and Helen Anne didn't want bad blood between them. When she turned her attention back to Jeremy, she said, "We need to talk privately."

"Neither the time nor place."

"I'm not asking, Jeremy. I'm telling you we need to talk. Now."

"Vikki and I will find seats," Rachel said, whisking into the confrontation with a sureness that bolstered Helen Anne.

"Fine," he said with a huff. "But make it quick. I'm not going to miss Macy taking the field." Like he was father of the year. What a joke! He'd missed more games than Helen Anne could count. But she wasn't interested in arguing the past; she was here to advocate for the future.

She watched her sister lead a slightly wary Vikki away, and when they were too far to hear a word, she said, "I'm in love with Giovanni Caceres."

"Jesus," he said disgustedly, and Helen Anne bristled. "You really know how to pick 'em."

"I know," she said, laughing, clearly referring to him. "Fourteen years married to a man who didn't respect me or treat me the way a husband should treat a wife. I hope to God you treat Vikki better than that. And if you don't, I will personally lead her to a divorce attorney. You may have been able to steamroll me in the settlement, but I won't let you steamroll her."

He looked a little stricken. "You're crazy."

"Maybe I am. Who knows? But if I am, you should be worried, because I'm sick and tired of being pushed around, Jeremy. I'm sick of being afraid of some abstract punishment you're about to levy. I'm done. I'm over your threats. You and I both know you pushed Giovanni before he ever swung at you. My guess is the D.A. knows it too, and that's why he hasn't taken things further."

He scoffed. "You don't know what you're talking about."

"But I do." The calm, cool voice was the last voice Helen Anne expected to hear. And Jackie Reed's intimidating face was the last face Helen Anne expected to see. She glared at Jeremy from overtop the hood of the full-size SUV that was blocking her sedan from view. "A little over a year ago I had security cameras installed at all entrances at my house. To protect your father, of course." She threw out that last bit to Helen Anne. "Just the other day, I had a copy of the recording from the picnic sent to the police station. To protect Giovanni, of course."

Helen Anne's heart contracted, squeezing the air from her lungs. *Of course.* Her legs went weak, and she locked her knees to keep her balance. She had never loved her mother more.

"We'll see you at the field," Jackie said, completely composed as if she'd never dropped a bomb, and then she disappeared behind the SUV, probably to retrieve Danny.

When Helen Anne's shock faded, she glanced at Jeremy, whose mouth hung open. There was a greenish cast to his face.

She laughed, and that startled him. "You look scared," she said. "Good. You should be scared. And I'll tell you something that should terrify you. I've been talking to my lawyer. If you continue to badmouth Giovanni and threaten to alter the custody agreement, I'll have no choice but to open up about everything. I have journals, Jeremy. Every horrible word you've ever said. I have therapy records from our marriage, as far back as our fifth anniversary. And you know what I learned? A therapist's professional opinion of an emotionally volatile relationship weighs much heavier on a judge than the juvenile record of an otherwise faultless man."

He said nothing. He simply stared at her as if he'd never seen her before, and the rush was incomparable.

Life coursed through her veins as she lifted her face to the sun. "I'm glad we had this talk." Finally. And now there was nothing left to say. At least not to him.

She turned and strode confidently away without a backward glance. The gravel crunching beneath her flats was the only proof she wasn't actually floating over the ground.

She'd done it. She'd finally stood up to the man who'd stolen all those years.

A few feet from the snack bar, she heard him behind her. "You, uh, you never told Macy about any of that. Did you? The therapy. The … "

She spun on him. "No, Jeremy. I wouldn't do that to her. I saw how upset she was when she overheard you call Giovanni a scumbag. I would never stoop that low. For some unfathomable reason, she loves you, and I would like to keep it that way. For her sake. But trust me, if you ever do anything to compromise her love, I will destroy you."

He stuttered. "I didn't mean for her to hear that. About Giovanni. I was talking to Vikki in private. I was frustrated. I didn't mean for Macy to hear it."

"But she did. So you should probably apologize for that. Profusely. Then you should apologize to Giovanni."

She saw her mother and father and Rachel and Vikki in the distance and smiled and waved. "Let's go," she said, making her way toward them. "We have a game to catch."

And for the first time in forever, Jeremy Gardner fell into line behind her.

• • •

"This is kind of like a double header," Macy said thoughtfully as she and Helen Anne raced toward Federal Field for the Aces' 7:05 game.

Macy was still dressed in her baseball uniform, because she'd refused to be late. Knowing what Helen Anne knew about the pending minor-league offer, tonight would be bittersweet. But after everything, she refused to be melancholy. Her time with Giovanni had changed her into a woman who was too proud to pout about golden opportunities, and that was exactly what Giovanni was being given by the Orioles affiliate.

At the stadium, Helen Anne and Macy settled into their usual seats behind home plate. Macy clutched her trusty glove and bounced her legs while she waited for the Aces to file into the dugout. A few players made the trek from the locker rooms beyond the outfield wall sooner than expected. They lined up for autographs, drawing in the few straggling fans that had been gathered around Helen Anne and Macy.

Macy joined them. And while Helen Anne watched her little girl pass her prized mitt to a new third baseman, Rosa Caceres slipped into Macy's seat.

"You need to go to the locker room now," Rosa said.

Helen Anne made a face. "Excuse me?"

"Right now. Before the game. My brother needs to talk to you. I'll stay with your little girl until you get back."

"Oh, I don't know about that." Helen Anne looked at her daughter, who was now in line for an autograph from a member of the opposing team. "Can't I talk to him after the game?"

"Only if you want him to play like crap." Rosa tugged on her arm. "He can't play when he's worried about something. So please, go. He needs to talk to you."

"I know what he's worried about," Helen Anne said sadly, finally giving in to the inevitable. "This is about him leaving."

Rosa shook her head. "You don't know everything, and you're wasting time. Go. I promise you, you'll thank me."

Something in the way Rosa said it made Helen Anne stand. She smoothed her linen shorts with shaky hands and said, "I won't be long. Please keep an eye on her."

All the way to the locker room, Helen Anne debated between going through with this pregame meeting and telling him, once and for all, she loved him or turning around and dealing with everything after the game. As she walked, she composed multiple texts letting him off the hook, congratulating him on the expected offer, and saying they would celebrate after the game—if he was available and wanted to. But she didn't send a single one. Instead, when she reached the long corridor, she found him crouched against the wall outside the locker room with his hands over his face.

"Gio?" she asked, concerned.

"You came!" He hopped to his feet in one strong fluid motion and grabbed her by both hands, pulling her into a nearby equipment room.

He let go of her and closed the door behind him, his eyes as wild as his smile. "I had to see you. I had to tell you. I figured it all out."

Her heart fell, but still she reveled in his unbridled joy. "I know you did. I'm so happy for you. You're going to make your family so proud. You're going to be the greatest centerfielder the Orioles have … "

"No. No. No." He reached for her again, squeezing her hands as he coaxed her closer. "I'm the greatest centerfielder the Aces have ever seen, and that's enough. For my family and me. I figured out the other part, the part that's going to make me enough for you."

She gasped. "What?"

"I love you," he said, loud and clear. "I love Macy, too. I want to dance with you and laugh with you and talk to you and be at all her games. I want to come home from every road trip knowing you're waiting for me. When I asked you what you wanted, you said everything, and I want to be the man who gives it to you, but I need to finish grad school first. Rosa is helping me look into online programs. I'm going to play for the Aces as long as I can, but while I travel and in the off-season, I'm going to get a master's degree in counseling so I can spend the rest of my life helping kids who were bullied like Macy and me." The sincerity in his gaze intensified as he brought their intertwined hands to rest against his heart. "But mostly, if you want me, I'm going to spend the rest of my life loving you."

Tears sprang in her eyes, and she threw her arms around his neck. "I want that. I want you."

He wrapped her up and rocked her back and forth. "I love you," he said again, his voice a harsh whisper, and then he repeated the words in Spanish and she opened her mouth to his neck, planting sweet kisses on his hot skin until she reached his mouth.

"I love you, too," she said. "So much."

"Caceres, are you in there?" The voice mixed with a pounding on the door.

"Be right out, Coach," he said, smiling down at her.

"You have five minutes to get your ass in that dugout or I'm giving your spot away."

In the spirit of urgency, Helen Anne tried to break from his arms, but Giovanni kept her pressed against him.

"Not yet," he whispered, inching his mouth closer to hers.

"You heard what he said. You're going to lose your spot."

"For one game. And it would be worth it. You're worth it." He kissed her again, long and lingering. When they finally broke free he stroked her cheek and stared at her for the longest time.

"What are you thinking?" she asked, her voice the softest whisper.

"I was thinking about something I told Macy the day I broke your windshield. The secret to hitting a ball out of the park is finding your sweet spot." He drew her lips to his again. "You're mine, Helen Anne. You're mine."

Acknowledgments

Tara, you were right. (You're always right.)

Lucianna, you planted this seed over dinner years ago, when we couldn't get Doc to try salsa dancing. (But one of these days …) Thanks to you (and your *papá*) for answering my questions.

Chris, you've been an inside source for baseball information multiple times now, and I'm grateful for all your experiences. (You really should write a book.) Thank you for always honestly and enthusiastically sharing your story with me.

And Doc, I might not have as many years on you as Helen Anne has on Giovanni, but thanks for giving this older woman a chance. A little bit of us is in every book I write.

About the Author

Elley Arden is a born-and-bred Pennsylvanian who has lived as far west as Utah and as far north as Wisconsin. She drinks wine like it's water (a slight exaggeration), prefers a night at the ballpark to a night on the town, and believes almond English toffee is the key to happiness. Elley writes books with charming characters, emotional stories, and sexy romance. For a complete list, visit www.elleyarden.com.

The Change Up
Elley Arden

Rachel Reed sat at her sleek black desk in her corner office over-looking city hall, complete with its statue of William Penn, and tried not to worry. Any time your boss came to town it was nerve-racking. This time wasn't any different. At least it shouldn't have been. Nothing had changed since the last time he'd been here. All systems were go on the abandoned warehouse being converted into residential space. Closings were complete on the land assemblage in downtown Philadelphia, and tenants in all ten buildings were being relocated efficiently.

She maniacally strummed her squared-off fingernails on the desk. *Think, think, think.* Was she missing anything? Was there any reason he'd be back in town so soon after his last visit? Had she made a mistake?

She just about shattered the intercom button with an overenthusiastic press as she summoned her executive assistant, Liv Butler, into the office.

"What's up?" Liv asked, bright and confident, like any young and hungry EA should be.

"Something is wrong," Rachel said, clicking through screen after screen of monthly status reports. "I can feel it. We've met all our objectives, correct?"

"Yep," Liv said, her face in her tablet. "Wait. Maybe he's coming in for your birthday. The big four-O."

Rachel looked up in time to see Liv's brows bob in jest and ignored it. Forty wasn't a big deal unless you were using it to measure professional success—as in being able to call yourself a multimillionaire by the time you turned forty. Rachel could do that, so forty could come and go without any fanfare, like all the rest. "My birthday is not for another week," she said dismissively. "Besides, that's too sentimental a reason for him to come in. We've never had that kind of relationship."

"Maybe he's retiring."

Never. He might've been sixty-five, but he had the focus and determination of a man half his age. "Liv, we're talking about a man who texts me at three a.m. to alter directives and clarify goals. He won't sleep, let alone retire." Although those texts had been far and few between lately.

Something was definitely wrong.

Rachel spent the next ninety minutes strumming like a madwoman, rereading texts and emails, replaying conversations in her head, trying desperately to come up with something—anything—that would warrant this visit. But everything was perfect on her end … until the intercom sounded again.

"They're here," Liv said.

They?

What the heck was Rachel in for?

The door opened, and her father walked in, followed by her mother. For as long as Rachel had been heading up the Philadelphia offices of Reed Commercial Real Estate Services, her mother had never stepped foot inside this building.

Maybe the impromptu visit was about her birthday after all. As weird as that would be.

Rachel stood, steadied her stride, muffled her surprise, and gave them the requisite greetings—a handshake for her father, who had been her business mentor and boss since she'd graduated from UPenn what seemed like a lifetime ago, and a hug for her mother, whom she saw once a year at Christmas—if her work schedule permitted. The greetings were even more stilted than usual.

"What brings you to Philadelphia?" she asked, knowing it wasn't business if her mother was in the mix. Jackie Reed preferred defined gender roles. Men worked. Women took care of them. Rachel couldn't think of a more miserable existence.

"Let's sit," her father said.

Those two little words tilted the world on its axis.

Rachel didn't hesitate to do as she was told. When your boss said jump, you asked how high. When your boss was your father, you didn't have to ask; you already knew. Still, her heart doubled its beat.

Once she was seated behind her desk, she studied her father, who couldn't seem to make eye contact with her. Danny Reed looked well: wrinkle-free skin a healthy shade of pink, salt-and-pepper hair as thick as always, tailored suit coat the perfect fit. When silence stretched on, she turned her attention to Jackie, who appeared every bit as put together as usual: neither a gray hair on her sleekly bobbed head nor a mark on her pancaked and painted face. Flowers and pastels were topped off with pearls. So why the long faces?

"We're sitting," Rachel said. "Now what?"

"Darling," Jackie started, finally looking at Rachel, only to be cut off by Danny.

"I have Alzheimer's," he said.

Rachel's breath hitched. Her father had never been one to beat around the bush. His assuredness and directness had made them all millions. But this time, she wished he'd built up to it. *Alzheimer's.* How was that possible? He looked great. He sounded great.

"Are you sure?" she asked.

"Positive," her mother said, tears glistening in her eyes, and Rachel had the foreign impulse to get touchy-feely. It didn't have time to flourish, though, because her father took control of the conversation again.

"We have work to do," he said, and he whipped out the leather-bound legal pad that accompanied him on every business trip.

But Rachel was still stuck on the news. *Alzheimer's*. When did he find out? What were his symptoms? How were they treating the disease?

"The attorneys should be here at four," he said. "You will have special power of attorney to make business deals on my behalf. These papers"—he slid the legal pad toward her—"detail my wishes. I simply ask that you follow them to a T."

She stared at the inch-thick stack of typed pages tucked in the inner pocket, her mind reeling. Surely power of attorney was a bit extreme. He sounded fine. He seemed competent.

"Rachel," her mother said. "Are you okay … with all of this?"

"Of course she's okay." Danny's brusque tone said the same thing it always did: Rachel was tough. His hand-groomed foot soldier. She could handle anything.

"I'm fine," Rachel said. "Just processing."

"Process this," her father said, tapping the folio again. "Everything you need to know is in there. I'll help as much as I can, but before it's too late, you need to have the legal power to execute these plans without my signature."

It made sense, except none of it made sense. He still didn't look like a man dealing with Alzheimer's disease. "Dad …" She paused as she leafed through the thick stack of pages.

And then something caught her eye. "You want me to sell the baseball team?" Oh, how she'd bit her tongue when she'd discovered three Christmases ago her father was considering a multimillion-dollar vanity project to bring independent baseball to her hometown of Arlington, Pennsylvania. The only thing that had kept her quiet at the time was her belief he would come to his senses and see how owning a barely professional baseball team in a league that had no affiliation with the MLB wasn't a good investment.

"But they haven't even had their first season." He was asking her to sell a team on speculation? She was a commercial real estate broker, not a magician.

More details flashed at her from the pages in her father's notebook. She was going to have to spearhead the remaining preparations for the inaugural season? "Dad," she said again, "I don't know anything about running a baseball team."

She'd been to her fair share of sporting events thanks to company season tickets and colleagues who needed to be schmoozed, and baseball was by far her favorite because of the atmosphere and the zen-like pace of the game, but enjoying the game was a far cry from understanding the business.

"You won't have to run it. The personnel we hire will run it. They are all listed in the folder." He sighed, a rare show of weakness, and she felt ridiculous for worrying about her workload when he was facing … Alzheimer's.

That word pulled the proverbial rug from underneath her.

"It's a lot," he continued. "I know it is. But it's probably the last thing I'm ever going to ask of you."

Rachel hated the lump that formed in her throat, hated that she couldn't think of confident words to displace it. She nodded.

"It's not the hereditary kind," her mother said suddenly. "So that's good news. Dr. Rictor said you and Helen Anne only have a slight increase in risk."

What a lovely thought. Not that on some level Rachel wasn't already worrying about it, but talking about it made it all the more real. *A slight increase in risk.* That was supposed to make her feel better.

It didn't. So she did what she always did when emotions threatened to swallow her whole. She looked at her father and, with a definitive nod and a slap of her hand to the leather-bound folder, said, "I can handle this. You have my word."

"I'm a sucker for second chance romances and *Running Interference* did not disappoint. This is my first Elley Arden read and I can guarantee it won't be my last. She has a unique writing style. Simple, yet strong with fluid and easy dialogue, you can't help but dive in and not come up until you're finished." — Eat Sleep Read Reviews

"I devoured the story ... Fun, sexy, and filled with smart ass side comments (and humor), this book is a great way to enter the world of the Cleveland Clash series." —4 stars, Art Books Coffee

The Kemmons Brothers Baseball Series

Save My Soul

Change My Mind

Heal My Heart

Take Me Out

Praise for the Kemmons Brothers series:

"Nel and Gray have a lot of fun and challenging things to face . . . You will fall in love with them both . . . For a fun, sweet and very entertaining read, don't miss *Change My Mind* by Elley Arden." —Harlequin Junkie

"...Elley Arden really manages to evoke a barrage of emotions in her readers. She really has a way of creating novels that will touch you." —Texas Book Nook

"This is one of those novels that combines a multiplicity of different elements, backgrounds, and social stigmas into a single whole that will take your breath away and leave you reeling. Arden's brilliant descriptions will paint a picture you won't soon forget."
—Pure Jonel

Harmony Falls Novels

Crashing the Congressman's Wedding

Battling the Best Man

Marrying the Wrong Man

Praise for the Harmony Falls series:

"The ending was my all-time favorite . . . This is definitely an AMAZING book that I recommend to all!" —Mamival's Books

"Good things come when you least expect it—at least I did with this book. I didn't expect to laugh, cry, and fall in love. But Elley Arden did those things to me, and after that short read, I think I'm coming back for more from this author." —Book Freak

Emerald Springs Legacy

Trouble Brewing

In the mood for more Crimson Romance?
Check out *Underground by Cecilia Johanna*
at CrimsonRomance.com.

Printed in the United States
By Bookmasters